CASSANDRA VEGA

Bound To Me

Copyright © 2024 by Cassandra Vega

All rights reserved. No part of this publication may be reproduced, stored or transmitted in any form or by any means, electronic, mechanical, photocopying, recording, scanning, or otherwise without written permission from the publisher. It is illegal to copy this book, post it to a website, or distribute it by any other means without permission.

This novel is entirely a work of fiction. The names, characters and incidents portrayed in it are the work of the author's imagination. Any resemblance to actual persons, living or dead, events or localities is entirely coincidental.

First edition

Cover art by Turning Pages Designs

This book was professionally typeset on Reedsy. Find out more at reedsy.com

*For the ones who survived—and the ones who didn't.*

# Please note:

This book contains heavy topics. A list of trigger and content warnings includes the following:
  Death of a parent/child finding dead parent
  Noncon
  BDSM
  Noncon scarification
  Knife play
  Blood play
  Degradation
  Abortion (mentioned, not detailed)
  Emotional, verbal, and physical abuse
  Suicide attempt
  Suicidal thoughts
  Restraints/captivity
  Stalking
  Emotional manipulation
  Somnophilia
  Violence
  Spitting
  Choking/breath play
  Forced orgasm
  Unaliving

**This book is not a manual for BDSM or any other sexual acts. Please do your own research and play responsibly.**

# Prologue

My shaky voice went unnoticed as my parents argued in the backyard. I swam with my floaties on my arms, trying to find my Barbie that floated off while I became distracted by their yelling. I didn't know what they were arguing about—my six year-old brain couldn't comprehend what "cheating" meant. We weren't playing Marco Polo, and we definitely weren't playing a game of Monopoly.

Daddy took Mommy's arm and pulled her inside. I was relieved that I couldn't hear the yelling anymore. I finally found Barbie near the little hole that sucked up all my other toys; Mommy said it was the filter to keep the pool clean. Then I heard my Mommy screaming and a loud bang. My little heart started pounding in my chest. I only heard that kind of banging during the Fourth of July, but it was bright and sunny outside.

"Mommy?" I called out.

There was no response. My daddy ran out with drops of red on his shirt.

"Jackie, honey, I have to go. Don't go inside, okay?" Daddy said, then he ran out the backyard gate.

Daddy was always coming and going like that so I didn't think anything of it. But he always ran like that before a policeman showed up at our door. Mommy always made me go to my room and she was always crying.

I wanted a snack, so I got out of the pool and called for Mommy. I heard sirens in the distance as I opened the back door.

"Mommy?" I called out.

I searched the kitchen and the living room but she wasn't there. I went down the hallway and into Mommy and Daddy's room. I saw the red stuff all over again. And I saw Mommy lying down on the bed. Even my little six year-old brain knew it then: my mommy was dead.

# Now

As I watched the snowflakes swirl and gently settle on the ground, I hugged my knees tightly, savoring the serene moment. Winter in New York City was a magical time, with its crisp air and blanket of white, a stark contrast to the mild, snowless winters of my California childhood.

I moved far away from my life in Los Angeles as soon as I could. I was in and out of foster homes from the age of six to sixteen. When I was seventeen, I ran away from my foster parents and took the Greyhound all the way from LA Union Station to Las Vegas. With a fake ID, I worked as an exotic dancer for two years as I saved all my money and lived around different hostels and stayed on friends' couches. I had to fend for myself, take care of myself, and when no one else was there for me, I had to pretend like I didn't want to give up and off myself. When I was nineteen, I hopped on a plane to New York City. It had been nine years since then, and I still didn't have my shit together. I wasn't sure if I ever would. Not after him.

I met Michael on a BDSM site when I was twenty-three, during my exploration phase. Before him, I had been with several men, and the sex was so dull that I thought that's just how it was meant to be. I always had to be drunk during those encounters because I was too self-conscious to open up otherwise. In truth, I often drank to numb the constant ache in my chest.

And then I met the perfect man: he was successful, gorgeous, and knew all the right things to say to keep little naive Jackie reeled in. I had always been attracted to older men and craved the sexual experiences they could bring. With him being in his early thirties, I expected a man his age to be beyond mind games and ready for a committed, healthy, loving relationship. He gave me the exact opposite.

I didn't realize I had been gnawing on my lip so hard that it was bleeding. Thinking about Michael sent me down a deep, destructive spiral, even after years of therapy. The irrevocable damage that he did to me would no doubt leave a permanent scar on my soul, just as his violence left permanent scars on my skin.

I jumped when my cell phone began vibrating on the couch beside me. Since it was an unknown number, I turned it over and ignored it. I looked back out the window, willing my mind to think about something else. YouTube—videos of cats always distracted me when I found myself spiraling. It was my new coping mechanism. Better than drinking, I suppose.

I opened the app just as a voicemail notification popped up. Out of curiosity, I listened, and once I heard it, I keeled over onto the floor and threw my phone at the wall. His voice would haunt me for the rest of my life, his scolding and yelling leaving deep wounds in my brain. I shook my head quickly, trying to get his words out of my mind.

*"Hello, my sweet Jackie. Daddy will be out soon...and I want to play."*

# Then

I waited at the subway station for the train that would take me home. I had just gotten off work from a trendy restaurant in Chelsea where I served. I hated all the stuffy Manhattanites who looked down at me like I was fucking dirt, but the tips were pretty good, so I didn't complain. I had just turned twenty-three and had already been working full-time for four years. I barely got by in my shared Park Slope apartment, but I refused to live anywhere besides Brooklyn. I wanted to be where all the fun was—all my friends had parties every other day, and we bar hopped up and down Brooklyn every weekend, all weekend. Even when my shift at the restaurant ended at 10 or 11 p.m., I'd still be ready to party for another four hours.

I was drinking too much. I knew I had a problem, but it was the only way to mask the enormous weight of loneliness and trauma I had felt for almost my entire life. I didn't know what it was like to feel any different. I had no idea if the pain would ever dull.

As I waited for the train, I swiped through the several dating apps I had on my phone. I met a few men off of them but they were all one night stands. I wasn't sure if I was looking for much else than that. The one I was the most curious about was the "kink friendly/BDSM" app. I had never done anything remotely kinky in my life, but I was dying to; I thought that was the missing piece in my sex life.

So many of the messages I received on the kink app were either from men who lived far out of the area or from those who sent unsolicited dick pics. Then a message from someone with the username YourNextDom popped up. Intrigued, I opened it.

**Hello, SweetJackie. I'm Michael. You're beautiful.**

I clicked on his profile picture. *Holy fucking shit. He can't be real. He has to be fake.* He was easily the most gorgeous man I'd ever seen. I skimmed through his pictures and he even posted a shirtless mirror selfie. My pussy pulsed. *God damn.*

**Hello, Michael. I don't think you're real,** I wrote back.

He immediately responded: **That's not a very sweet thing to say, SweetJackie. Why do you think that?**

I smiled as I replied: **Because you're too fucking hot. A man that looks like you doesn't exist.**

My heart fluttered when he messaged back: **You better watch your mouth. You could get punished for speaking that way to me.**

I put my phone away, blushing. The train had arrived, and I had no idea how to respond to him. If he was real, I was in big trouble.

I walked out of the subway station, feeling my phone vibrating in my pocket. It was Michael. **I don't like waiting, SweetJackie.** I decided to be brave; I had nothing to lose. I wrote back: **Prove you're real and I'll beg on my knees for forgiveness.** *I can't believe I just wrote that. But he's not real—he can't be. I have nothing to worry about.*

My heart nearly leapt out of my chest when I saw a video request from him. I stood at the foot of the stairs leading up to my apartment. *Fuck, I look like shit.*

I hesitantly answered, and his face appeared on the screen.

"Hello, sweet Jackie. Is this enough proof for you?" He had an Irish accent and his eyes were a dark, deep gray. His face must have been chiseled by God himself.

"Um." I smiled as I looked at my stunned face at the bottom of the screen. "Yes. Yes, it is."

He gave me a quick smile. "So, when do I get to see you on your knees?"

# Now

I pulled my heavy carry-on luggage behind me as I anxiously searched for my seat. After the call from Michael, I changed my number and quit my job. Getting a last minute ticket to LA was pricey, but I needed to get out of New York City; I had too many horrid memories that I'd never be able to escape. LA was the only other place I knew. I hadn't been back since I boarded that Greyhound bus when I was seventeen. I didn't know how much had changed in eleven years. Were east Hollywood and Silverlake still trendy? Was the valley still the porn capital of LA? Was Burbank, the place I lived for six years with my mom and dad, going to send me into a panic attack?

I found my seat towards the back of the plane and quickly made eye contact with an attractive man sitting directly next to mine. I looked away and kept my eyes on the floor; I was not in the mood to be ogling a gorgeous man like him. The last one I was with had tortured me, and I would never trust a beautiful exterior again. In fact, I hadn't been with anyone since him. I didn't think I'd ever be with anyone again, and I was okay with that.

I feebly lifted my carry-on to the only available space across from my seat. My cheeks burned with embarrassment as I struggled to push it into place.

"May I help?" a deep voice beside me asked.

I quickly glanced over to see the attractive seat neighbor. His light, kind eyes crinkled slightly at the corners as he smiled. His salt-and-pepper curly hair was gelled to the side. *Great, and he's older. Just my type.*

"No, thanks. I got it." I turned away, continuing to push my bag, out of breath. He stayed beside me as I strained, and I wanted to cry. *I can't fucking do anything myself.* "Okay. I'll take the help," I finally said, holding up the bag to keep it in place.

I glanced over at him as he smiled and placed his hands next to mine, easily securing the bag in the overhead bin. I could see his muscles contracting beneath his long-sleeved T-shirt.

"Thank you." I gave him a quick smile before looking down, waiting for him to move.

"No problem," he replied, his deep, velvety voice stirring a wave of desire within me.

I watched his feet as he walked to the other side of the aisle and hesitated to move. *I will not let myself become obsessive and controlled again. I will not give in.*

I quickly looked up and saw Hot Nice Older Man settling into the window seat beside mine. I took a deep breath as I moved to my seat, feeling his gaze melt my insides. *So fucking typical, Jackie.* I hated that my harsh inner dialogue was narrated by Michael.

"You going to visit somewhere or heading back home?"

He was looking at me out of the corner of my eye. I wasn't sure I could easily make small talk with someone so good-looking.

"I'm, uh, moving back home. To LA. From here," I stammered, glancing at him briefly before looking at the back of the seat in front of me. An ad for the airline played silently on a small screen.

"Oh? How long have you lived here?" he asked, effortlessly drawing me into conversation.

I sighed. "Nine years." I nodded and gave him a stiff smile, still struggling to make eye contact.

"I'm headed back home. I have family around here," he offered, his tone friendly despite my short responses.

As the flight attendants began their safety demonstration, I focused intently ahead, hoping the gorgeous man would take the hint and stop talking. I didn't want him to waste his breath on me.

"Where in LA are you from?" he asked, oblivious to my silent plea.

"I'm sorry. I'm sure you're very nice and just trying to make small talk during this long flight, but I'm in no shape to talk about myself," I snapped, immediately regretting how I was speaking to Hot Nice Older Man.

I finally made eye contact with him for more than a second, and the unexpected warmth that spread through me was both hot and startling. I hadn't felt this way about anyone since Michael. This was dangerous. His widened, sad eyes quickly looked away, and he nodded.

"I'm sorry. I understand."

My heart leapt into my throat. I felt like shit. But I couldn't give any man attention, and I definitely didn't want his. Okay, maybe I *did* want his, but it would be a waste of time. He wouldn't want someone with both literal and figurative scars and a dark, shitty history like mine.

Despite him leaving me alone, I felt a need to defend myself.

"I'm sorry. I didn't mean to snap. But I've been through hell and back, and I don't want to waste your time."

He gave me a small smile and shook his head. "No need to apologize. I completely understand," he said, then lowered his voice. "However, I don't think any time with you would be a waste."

I may have gasped quietly.

"Sorry." He smiled shyly. "I'll leave you alone now." He turned his head and looked out the window.

*Good. That will be the best decision you've ever made, Hot Nice Older Man.*

I sank lower in my seat, put on my noise-canceling headphones, and closed my eyes, not once falling asleep.

# Then

I had never been so nervous in my life. I was about to go on a date with easily the hottest guy I'd ever seen. He was ten years older than me and an "experienced dom." He seemed to like that I was inexperienced; he said he wanted to "show me the ropes." We agreed to meet in a neutral setting to see if we hit it off, and then go from there. I wasn't sure what that meant exactly, but I was pretty sure I'd do anything he wanted.

I stepped into a sleek hotel bar in the East Village, far from my usual spots. The place was crowded, with a variety of people sitting at the bar and at tables in the middle of the room. I awkwardly stood at the entrance, scanning the room for any sign of him. *What if he stood me up? What if this was all just a cruel joke? Why would he want someone like me anyway?*

Suddenly, I felt a hand on my elbow. I turned to find him standing there: short, brown wavy hair, dark gray eyes, and a stubble of facial hair. He was even hotter in person. *Holy fucking hell.* He smiled at me tenderly before speaking.

"Sweet Jackie?"

My heart dropped to my core, and my pussy seemed to swallow it whole.

"Y-yeah. And you're Michael?" I managed to stammer.

He raised his eyebrows slightly. "If you're lucky, you'll be calling me Daddy by the end of the night."

My mouth dropped open, and I felt my knees buckle.

"This way. I have a table reserved for us." He extended his hand toward me.

My shaky hand took his, and he led us to our table. I felt underdressed in my skinny jeans and white silky blouse; he wore black pants with a button-up shirt and nice shoes. I couldn't stop staring at the back of his head. When we reached our table, he pulled my chair out for me. *He's handsome and a gentleman? I think I've found my future husband.* I smiled at him as I sat and watched him take his seat. I literally couldn't take my eyes off him. When he glanced up after sitting, my cheeks burned with embarrassment.

"So, sweet Jackie. Do you believe I'm real now?" He was teasing me.

I looked down at the table and laughed. "Yes. You're very real."

I hesitantly looked up. His gaze was almost too intense to bear; it had become serious and penetrating.

"I have a few things I should mention before we continue. First, if we move forward, you'll need to sign an NDA. I'm a very private person," he began.

I shifted in my seat; this was *one way* to start a date.

"Secondly, this isn't a date. This is a meeting to see if we're compatible. I don't date. I only have relationships with my subs in the bedroom."

My heart sank.

"Lastly, if you agree to be my submissive, you'll be my only submissive. I expect you to have no other relationships with anyone else."

*I started to chew on my bottom lip. What am I getting myself into? Do I really want this? I don't even know if I'll like being a submissive.*

"Okay." I nodded.

Michael smiled again. "Perfect. Can I get you a drink?"

"Yes, please," I answered immediately.

He waved the server over. "We'll take a bottle of your finest champagne."

I looked back down at the table, unable to maintain eye contact.

"No need to be nervous, Sweet Jackie. I will take good care of you."

I glanced back up at him, hanging on his every word.

"Can we have, like, a trial period? To make sure this is what I want?" I asked hesitantly.

He chuckled lightly. "Of course. And you won't be bound to me in any way. You'll always have the opportunity to leave, whenever you want."

I nodded, feeling a bit relieved.

The server brought a bottle of champagne and two flutes. He quickly poured our glasses and walked away.

Michael eyed me intently. "Whenever you're ready, we can go upstairs and start your trial period."

I almost choked on my champagne. I caught my breath and set my flute down.

"I think I'm ready now."

# Now

We pulled into LAX under a dark and cloudy night sky. Of course, I had to arrive during the only period of rain forecasted for five days straight in sunny Southern California. Nice Hot Older Man respected my wish not to be bothered. He nodded to me when I returned from the bathroom, but that was it. I began to regret my decision to dismiss him; I knew absolutely no one in California anymore. Well, except for my dad out in the desert, who was rotting away in prison. *Maybe Nice Hot Older Man could be my emergency contact or something.*

"Um, sorry for...being so rude," I said, turning to him as we waited our turn to exit the plane.

He smiled and shook his head. "You weren't rude. I understand needing privacy."

I quickly smiled back. "Okay. Thanks." I felt my cheeks burning again. I hadn't had this much conversation with a man this gorgeous in years.

He cleared his throat as I turned my eyes back to the front of the plane.

"If you ever feel like... maybe you don't want so much privacy, could I give you my card?"

I turned back to him, feeling like my eyes were popping out of my head.

"Uh—"

"No, I'm sorry. That's too forward, isn't it? Now I feel like a creep," he responded immediately, clearly embarrassed.

"No, it's fine." I laughed. His modesty was endearing. "Sure, I'll take your card."

He smiled again. I couldn't let this man into my life—I would ruin him. Or vice versa. But I could be kind and flatter myself.

He reached for his wallet in his back pocket and pulled out his card. He handed it to me, and I immediately read it: "Elliott Walker. Behavioral Therapist."

I knew I looked up at him with a scowl on my face. He began to laugh.

"Sorry, I'm not giving you my card as a potential client. I was, um...if you ever want to get a drink or dinner or something." He seemed nervous, but he surely must've done that all the time. I'm sure he had many "potential clients."

"Thanks." I waved his card in my hand and stood up, making my way out to the aisle.

I was so lost in my thoughts that I had forgotten all about my overhead bag. I turned around and Elliott was taking it down for me effortlessly.

"Fuck," I said under my breath. *He must think I'm a real fucking mess.* "Thanks. Again." I smiled as I took my bag from him.

I quickly turned around and nearly ran out to the terminal.

I found my baggage claim area and waited as the carousel began to unload bags. I glanced down at my phone, not even really sure why I was checking it. I didn't give anyone my new number; I wasn't sure if I would. Maybe LA would be my fresh start and absolve me of all my trauma from New York, even though my trauma started right here in this very city. *I'm never going to be a normal person. Maybe I can at least pretend.*

I saw Elliott approaching the carousel and looked back down at my phone, hoping to avoid him; I couldn't keep making an asshole out of myself, and he seemed to just bring it out of me. *The nicest guy I've ever met, and I can't even be nice to him. I am obviously unwell.*

I glanced up at the bags making their way around the loop and realized Elliott had gone to the opposite side of where I stood, respectfully keeping his distance. Or maybe he just knew I was fucking crazy and wanted to stay the hell away from me.

I grabbed my large purple suitcase, propped my carry-on bag on top of it, and wheeled it out the door. The sound of traffic immediately filled my ears; even at 9 p.m. on a weekday, the airport was filled with non-stop traffic. In the minute I had been outside, the rain escalated from a light sprinkle to a torrential downpour as I desperately searched for the shuttle to my hostel in East Hollywood. I felt like a foreigner already—I didn't know where the fuck I was going or how to get there.

Someone suddenly bumped into my shoulder, and as we both turned, he apologized. Naturally, it was Elliott.

"Oh, I'm so sorry—uh." He searched my face as he gestured towards me, as if my panicked expression would tell him my name.

"Jacqueline." My full name sounded more sophisticated than Jackie, and I had no idea why I wanted to impress this man.

"Like Jackie O?" He smiled, his hair dripping wet as we stood under an overpass.

Exactly like it; of course, my parents thought it would be so cute to name their daughter Jacqueline with the last name Olsen. Jackie O was my nickname for many years in school.

"Yeah." I smiled and shrugged.

He looked around. "Are you waiting for a bus?"

*Run for your life, Elliott*, my internal Michael monologue yelled.

"Yeah," I replied, glancing around, still uneasy about making eye contact with him.

"Oh, um…I can give you a ride?" he started, but his face fell instantly. "Actually, let me just stop my recurrent creepiness right here. I'm sure you don't want a ride from a stranger." He raised his eyebrows at me with a disarming smile.

I nodded. I may have been barely living, but I didn't want to get murdered just yet.

"You're fine." I shook my head. "I mean—it's fine. I think this is my bus anyway." I nodded over at an approaching bus.

He nodded back. "Okay. I hope you get to your destination safely." He smiled again. "I hope to see you again, Jacqueline." He turned and walked away into the rain.

I stood there staring at him until the bus zoomed right past me.

*Off to a great start already, Jackie O.*

# Then

I nervously signed the NDA; I never thought I'd ever have to sign one, let alone before having sex with someone. I gulped down another glass of champagne and sat on the bed as Michael took his time in the bathroom. I looked around the room—it was definitely a nice hotel, a place I'd never be able to afford. By the looks of Michael, he seemed to be unfazed by the cost of anything. I stood up and walked over to the window, eager to check out the view. We were high up, almost to the top floor, and I could see all around the East Village and the surrounding neighborhoods.

I jumped, startled, when Michael finally walked out of the bathroom. I quickly turned around, and he was slowly walking toward me, his clothing removed except for his boxer briefs, and he held rope in his hand. I grasped onto the window frame as I took him all in—his pictures did him absolutely no justice. I had never been with anyone remotely that attractive. I could tell by the look on his face that he knew what I was thinking.

"Take off your clothes, sweet girl," he ordered gently, now only standing a couple of feet in front of me.

We hadn't even kissed yet—he already wanted me to take my clothes off?

"I'm not going to ask again, Jackie. Take your clothes off.

Now."

A mixture of fear and arousal rose from deep within my chest. I shakily began to unbutton my jeans while simultaneously kicking off my Converse. I couldn't look at him; he was too fucking hot for me to even think if I made eye contact with him.

"Look at me while you undress," he demanded, his voice deep and gravelly, a stark contrast from where he started.

My eyes darted to his. I saw the desire in his eyes as his erection grew. I continued to pull off my shirt as my jeans fell to the floor; I was so glad I wore matching underwear.

"Your bra and underwear now."

He waited as he slowly eyed me up and down.

I almost spoke to object, but I couldn't form any words. I unhooked my bra and slipped down my underwear.

A smile arose on his face as he looked me up and down again.

"What a beautiful, soft body you have," he praised, stopping at my eyes.

That was not a compliment I had ever received. *What does a soft body mean?*

"Thank you." I felt my eyebrows twitch as I spoke, unsure of myself.

He started to walk around me, surveying my body. If any other man did that to me, I would have pushed him away and run out of the room. But there was something about him; not just his looks, but his dominance and the power he exuded.

"I'm going to tie this rope around your wrists behind your back. Do you consent?" he asked as he stood behind me.

I turned my head, my heart racing wildly. *What the fuck have I gotten myself into?* "Yes."

*Oh God, I'm gonna get murdered, aren't I?* I didn't think I would even be mad if he murdered me—he was too good-looking.

## THEN

My chest rose and fell quickly as he began to bind my wrists together.

"Your safe word is 'red.' You can use it when I'm doing something to you that you don't want or like," he explained.

My heart was racing. "Okay." I nodded, although he was still behind me.

"And you will now refer to me as Daddy. Do you understand?"

"I—yes, Daddy." *Holy fuck, why is that turning me on so much?* I hadn't called anyone daddy except for my actual dad, and that hadn't been in almost twenty years.

He chuckled softly. "You're a quick learner, my sweet girl. Do you want to please Daddy?"

My breathing hitched. I somehow wanted that more than anything in the world.

"Yes, Daddy."

He finished tying my wrists together and stood in front of me. "Good. Then get on your knees." His voice was so deep and God, that accent drove me insane.

I quickly dropped to my knees. I knew that whatever he told me to do, I'd do it.

He stared down at me and gently put his hand to my cheek.

"Beg for Daddy's cock."

The arousal I felt between my thighs as I stared up at him had me instantly begging.

"Please, Daddy. I want your cock," my shaky voice let out.

His eyes set ablaze. "What a good girl."

He pulled down his boxer briefs and let his hard cock spring free in my face. I instantly gasped—I only saw cocks like his in porn.

"Suck," he ordered.

I opened my mouth wide and pressed my lips to the head of

his cock. He pulled away quickly and shook his head.

"Eyes on me."

I shifted my gaze to his and took him into my mouth, moans escaping my throat as I found a steady rhythm. He watched me as he took his hand behind my head, holding my hair.

He smiled down at me. "Just like that, baby."

I had never been so proud of myself in my entire life. I was pleasing this beautiful man and his praise sent a chill down my spine.

He quickly pulled away and walked behind me, taking my bound hands and lifting me to my feet. He guided me to the desk in front of the bed and easily picked me up and sat me down on it.

"I'm going easy on you, baby. This is just a taste of what you'll get."

He pushed me onto my back on top of my bound wrists and lifted my hips in the air. His strong arms held on to the back of my thighs and he was suddenly inside of me. My whole body trembled as his cock pushed deeply in and out of me, every nerve in my pussy feeling like a ticking time bomb. I was on the verge of my orgasm when he stopped and pulled out of me.

"From now on, you need to ask permission to come," he said before plunging himself back into me.

The build to my orgasm was quick as he continued and I knew my release was approaching.

"Please Daddy," I moaned. "Can I come?"

"Yes, my sweet girl. Come all over Daddy's cock."

His words sent my pussy into a deep, pulsing wave of release, the moans coming out of my mouth sounding foreign to my ears. I had never felt an orgasm as intensely as this one and I chased another as I lifted my hips up and down.

He pulled out of me quickly. "Just one, baby. Now you need to take care of Daddy. If you're good, I'll make you come again." He pulled me upright and I felt dizzy and high from his cock.

He stood me up then pushed me down onto the bed, face first, with my legs still dangling over the edge. His hands pulled my legs apart before he stuck a finger in my ass and I gasped with surprise.

"Has anyone been inside my sweet Jackie's ass?" His hot breath was against my ear.

"No," I breathed out.

There was a sudden slap to my ass that prompted a surprised scream from my throat.

"Try answering that again, baby girl," he demanded.

"No—no, Daddy," I corrected myself.

"Good," he said, then I heard him spit before it ran down to my ass.

His cock was now at the tip of my asshole and I began to tremble. I was nervous about his size and the fact that I had never done anal before. He pushed himself into me quickly and deeply, the pain unbearable as he continued to plunge inside of me.

"Stop. Stop! Re—red, red, red," I cried out. "Please! Stop!" He covered my mouth with one hand while the other began to rub my clit, his pounding never ceasing. The pain was still searing through me but my pussy started to tremble under his touch, an orgasm approaching. My cries turned into a loud moan of pleasure as I came and he started to grunt loudly as he slowed his hips. My crying returned as my orgasm slowed. I had never felt more violated or used before; I used my safe word and he quieted me, not giving a fuck. And it fucking *hurt*.

"Untie me. Please," I sobbed, his cock still in my ass.

"Oh baby, why are you crying?" He pulled out of me and turned me over.

His eyes were staring down at me while he hovered over me.

"I told you to stop," I said between hitched breaths.

He smiled and kissed my cheek atop the tears flowing down. "Baby girl, you're all mine now. You don't get a say in this."

I looked up at him with fear consuming me. I wanted to scream and kick at him. I wanted to yell for help. But I didn't do any of those things.

"I'm yours?" I whispered.

He grinned triumphantly. "Yes, baby. Come on, let me run you a bath."

He lifted me up and began to remove the rope from my wrists. I almost thought I made it all up in my head, that I hadn't just been crying and begging for him to stop. It was as if that had all disappeared once he told me I was his.

He turned me around and gently took my face in his hands. "If you continue to submit yourself to me, without misbehaving, I will always make you feel good and you will always be mine."

I closed my eyes and leaned my cheek into his hand.

"Yes, Daddy."

# Now

I checked into the East Hollywood hostel in a shared dorm room where I would be staying for the foreseeable future. It was all I could afford until I got a job. I had a small savings that I reserved for an emergency such as this, and it would probably only get me by for about a month if I only ate Top Ramen for every meal. And then I would be homeless. I figured that was better than staying in New York City, where I would constantly be reminded of Michael and where he would probably end up finding me once he got out of prison. I didn't want to know what he'd do to me if he saw me again.

There were three bunk beds with only one space available on a bottom bunk by the window. The place wasn't as bad as I thought it would be—it was clean, the staff was friendly, and there were a lot of amenities like free breakfast and a common room with couches, a TV, and computers with WiFi. But I still had to share a room with five other women and question if my belongings would be safe in the little locked closet I had. I had been robbed of things in some of the many hostels I stayed in before. My room almost reminded me of my stay in a "teen mental health hospital" when I was sixteen, right before I ran away. My foster parents decided that my sneaking out and partying with friends meant I had psychological problems.

I knew that I had problems, but the least of them were my drinking and partying.

I made myself comfortable as I lay in my bunk, applying for any job I could find. I hoped my extensive restaurant history, especially in New York City, would take my resume to the top of the candidate list.

And then my mind wandered to Elliott. I wondered where he lived. Probably somewhere like Beverly Hills or somewhere nice in the valley. And of course, I had to google him. I easily found his website where his picture popped up, his bright blue eyes staring into mine. He was clean-shaven and looked extremely professional, a stark contrast to the relaxed, natural demeanor I saw at the airport. I decided to check Instagram; maybe I could find out more about his life on there. I found him again but his profile was private. *Damnit.* It was probably best though; I had an obsessive, addictive personality, and I needed to stay away from him. I couldn't let myself get close to anyone. I would never be able to trust anyone anyway.

I had a couple of calls the next day for interviews. I took the bus to each interview and reminded myself that I needed to get my license if I was going to make it in LA. A couple of days had passed, and there were still no callbacks. I started to panic. *Why couldn't I have just stayed in New York? Sure, everything there reminded me of Michael, but I could have just moved to a different neighborhood. I didn't need to move across the country, did I?*

I hadn't had a drink in several months. I had tried countless times to quit on my own, even going to rehab a year before, but inevitably, I relapsed. There was still nothing else that could take away that dull ache in my chest. And being back in California felt lonely as fuck—I didn't know a single soul out here. I needed to mingle. *Fuck it, I'm going to a bar.*

## NOW

There were a lot of bars within walking distance in the neighborhood I was staying in. I found a cute little retro bar only about a three minute walk away. It gave classic Hollywood vibes; the 1920s Art Deco style was evident in the light fixtures, the bar backdrop, and even the sign for the place itself. There was a DJ playing modern music on the side, and in the crowd were a mixture of people: younger, older, hipsters, professionals. I made my way to the bar and looked over their menu as I sat on a stool. I was immediately approached by the bartender, a gorgeous blonde with matte red lipstick. She reminded me of Hana. My heart stung at the reminder of Michael again.

"What can I get you, babe?" she asked, a warm smile spread across her face.

"Um." I looked back down at the menu, its extensive cocktails making my head spin. "Can I just get like, a vodka seven?"

Her friendly grin grew wider. "Of course!" She walked away and started on my drink.

I grabbed my phone out of my purse and scrolled through apps, wondering whether or not to sign up for another dating app. *You fucking moron—look who you met last on a dating app.* I shook my head at myself. I was trying to work on talking nicely to myself, something I had worked on in therapy, but it was hard to focus on that when I was stressed and living in a place that felt foreign to me now.

"Your vodka seven, my dear." The bartender put my drink down in front of me. "Do you want to open a tab?"

I looked around and wondered how long I'd be staying. "Sure." I shrugged then dug for my card in my purse.

"Where are you visiting from?" she asked as she waited.

"Uh." I laughed. *Am I that obvious?* "I just moved here from New York City, but I grew up here," I explained.

"Oh, nice! Welcome back!" She walked away with my card.

I sighed heavily to myself as I took a gulp of my drink. Fuck, the burn down my throat to my stomach was such a nice feeling. I tugged on my sleeves, a nervous habit, always highly aware of the horrid scars on my body.

Someone to my right approached me. "Can I get you a drink?"

I glanced over and a bearded, nice-looking—albeit younger-looking—guy smiled at me. *I should say no, but I'm broke as fuck.*

"Sure." I smiled back.

"I'm Jesse." He stood closer to me; I immediately felt uncomfortable.

"Jackie." I nodded to him.

"Hey Zee, can I get this beautiful lady another one?" He waved over at the friendly, blonde bartender.

I looked over at her as she nodded.

"You live around here?" he continued.

I sighed, not nearly drunk enough to start the small talk flirting.

"Yeah." I was being vague as he inched closer.

Zee gave me my second drink and I gulped all of it down quickly. Jesse laughed and slammed his hand down on the bar, thoroughly entertained. *That makes one of us.*

"Damn, girl. Looking to get fucked up tonight?"

"Precisely. Preferably alone," I muttered, glancing over at Zee.

Jesse scoffed and slowly walked away. *Thank God he wasn't pushy.*

"You alright, babe?" Zee asked, a familiar look of concern on her face.

"Yeah. Can I get another?"

She looked down at my drink. "Sure."

I sighed as I tapped on my phone, my mind immediately wandering to Elliott. *God, he's so damn handsome.* I went to his private Instagram and hit "Follow." *This is such a bad idea. He's gonna know I've been stalking him.* I set my phone down and nursed my third drink after Zee set it down in front of me. My eyes quickly shot to the notification that Elliott had accepted my request and was now following me. I laughed, feeling tipsy and ready to flirt. I gasped when a message from him appeared: **Well hello there, Jacqueline. It's nice to see you again.** My heart began to race. *This is not a good idea to respond, especially while drinking.* I immediately typed back: **Hi Elliott. I guess it's apparent I've been stalking you. Sorry about that.** *Oh what a fucking idiot, Jackie.* I saw typing bubbles immediately appear. **Ha! That's not a bad thing. I'm really glad to hear from you. I thought I'd never see you again.** My heart sunk. *Fuck, no no no. I can't do this.* My fingers had a mind of their own as they typed: **I want to see you again. But I'm really a fucked up mess, and you will probably run for the hills once you really know me. Especially as a therapist.** I set my phone down and put my hands to my forehead. My phone buzzed only seconds later and I quickly read his message: **I'd like to figure that out on my own. Everyone is a mess to some degree.** I shook my head, tears pooling my eyes. I gulped down my drink and began to type again: **No like, you don't understand. I have been traumatized. I will never be able to trust you. I don't want to do that to you. You're too nice.** I stared down at my phone as he started to type. **You don't have to tell me anything**

**you don't want to. However, I still want to see you again.** I groaned, finally letting tears fall down my cheeks.

"You okay?" Zee was standing in front of me behind the bar, the look of concern still on her face.

"I'm...no. I'm fine. I should go." I started to stand up.

"Hey, wait, your tab!"

I waited as she grabbed my card. She came back and held it out for me along with a receipt to sign.

"If you need someone to talk to, or just a friend, I'd be happy to hang out. My number is on the receipt." She smiled at me.

I nodded and gave the best smile that I could. "Thanks."

I walked out of the bar and my phone began to buzz in my purse. I stood against the wall, the cold air making my buzz feel even stronger. I pulled out my phone and almost had a heart attack: Elliott was calling me on Instagram. *Oh my God. Fuck it. Answer it!*

"Hey?" I answered hesitantly.

"Hey, Jacqueline. Are you okay?" There was concern clear in his voice.

I sighed. "Yeah. I'm just...I've been drinking. It was probably a bad idea to message you in this state," I admitted, shaking my head at myself.

There was a pause. "That's okay. Do you need help? Are you able to get home safely?"

I hated that I was already making this beautiful stranger worry about me.

"I'm walking back to my hostel right now. I'll be fine. Maybe a little hungover, but fine nonetheless." I began walking towards "home."

"You're staying in a hostel? Where?" he asked. "If you don't mind me asking. There's just...there's a lot of bad areas in LA.

I'm sure you know that."

I laughed to myself. "I do know that. It's fine, it's in East Hollywood. The Hollywood Hostel." *Am I secretly wanting him to find me?*

I heard him sigh. "Okay. Well…at least stay on the line with me until you get there."

I smiled to myself. "Okay, *dad,*" I teased, but it immediately stung. *Don't ever call a man dad or daddy again, you idiot.*

Elliott laughed. "You're right. I'm probably old enough to be your dad."

I stopped walking as I waited for the crosswalk to turn green.

"No, I doubt it. How old are you?" I asked curiously, then began to walk again.

"I'm forty-six.. I'm scared to ask how old you are. I'll feel like a *real* creep then," he teased.

*Oh God. He's older and smart and so fucking handsome.* "I'm twenty-eight. See, that's not creepy," I assured him with a smile on my face.

He groaned and I felt my pussy twitch. "Yes, it *is* creepy. I'm eighteen years older than you."

I bit my lip. I wanted him so badly. But I couldn't let it happen. Ever.

"If I say it's not creepy, it's not creepy. You should be flattered that a twenty-eight year old thinks you're hot." *Oh God, I did not just say that.* "I mean, you're—fuck." I laughed, my tipsiness at its height.

He laughed too. "Well, yes…I am *very* flattered. Especially coming from you."

I scoffed. "I'm sure you get that all the time." I was now at the front entrance of the hostel. "You must be swatting away the ladies like flies." *Fuck it, I can flirt;* that's all I could let myself do.

"Actually, not quite. I'm so busy that I don't have time to be...swatting ladies away." He laughed lightly. "But I could make the time for you."

The fire in my core dropped straight to my pussy. "You're gonna swat me away?" I teased.

He laughed again. "No, that's not what I meant. Jacqueline, I know you say you're a mess, but I'd love to see you again." His tone was earnest and sweet.

I shut my eyes tight. "I can't. I mean...I can be your friend, Elliott, but any more than that...I just can't." I felt like crying.

There was silence for a moment. "I *do* need more friends." There was a smile in his tone.

Another tug at my heartstrings. "Okay, well, *friend*. I made it back home. I'm safe for tonight."

He sighed. "Good. Can I call you again tomorrow?"

I bit my lip as I smiled. "Sure. I'd like that."

# Then

The need to feel like I belonged overpowered any reservations I had about Michael. I never had anyone tell me that I was *theirs*. I desperately wanted to be loved and needed. Once Michael said those words, something in my brain shorted, all logic was disregarded, and all I knew was that I needed to please him—to make him happy. I hadn't had a family or anything else that felt remotely like love in many, many years. I was abandoned and left to fend for myself. Now, someone was going to finally take care of me.

Michael didn't let me stay the night with him. He insisted that we shouldn't be sleeping together like that. I was hurt but I didn't question him—he knew what he was doing.

Over the next few days, I checked my phone every minute, waiting for his call or text. I was distracted at work, writing down wrong orders, getting yelled at and threatened to be fired. I didn't care anymore; all that I cared about was Michael. And when he finally called me four days later after I incessantly texted and called him, I left work early to go see him. Inevitably, I was fired.

I knocked at Michael's door as I cried. I was freaking out that I no longer had a job—how was I going to pay my rent? How was I going to live? I knew I wouldn't get a recommendation from the place I had just worked at for two years. *I am such a fucking idiot.*

"Oh, baby girl, what's wrong?" Michael answered the door and held me in his arms.

"I just got fired. They didn't understand that I needed to come see you *right now*," I cried into his chest.

Michael stroked my hair. "That's okay, sweet girl. I'll take care of you. You'll never have to worry about that again."

Oh, how I ate his words up.

"Really?" I looked up at him, my eyes burning from the makeup that ran into my eyes.

He smiled down at me. "Yes. Come in. Daddy needs you."

He tied my hands to the headboard after he stripped me slowly. I waited as he elaborately tied my ankles to the bottom of his bed frame. All I wanted was for him to be inside of me, to make me his again. I would never use my safe word again—I didn't want to upset him. If he hurt me again, I would be his good girl and let him hurt me.

"Are you going to behave tonight, baby?"

He walked around the bed as he surveyed my body.

"Yes, Daddy." I nodded eagerly.

"Is your pussy wet for Daddy?" He crawled onto the bed over me, his toned arms and abs contracting as his erection pressed against my stomach.

"Yes, Daddy," I answered again.

He licked his lips before he got to his knees and put his head between my thighs.

"Beg Daddy to lick your wet pussy," he demanded, his hot breath only inches away from my pulsing pussy.

I didn't hesitate. "Please, Daddy. Please lick my pussy," I moaned, straining my neck to watch him.

He suddenly buried his face into my pussy, his hands clenching onto my thighs as he licked his way around, tasting me. I felt warmth spread throughout my body as he circled my clit with his tongue and as he pressed two fingers inside of me.

"Oh my God," I called out, close to coming.

He suddenly pulled away from me and bit the inside of my thigh, hard. I screamed as he continued, drawing blood.

"Daddy!" I cried.

He stopped and looked up at me, his lips speckled with blood. "That's right. You'll never praise God in this room, only Daddy." Then he continued to lick my clit, quickly making me come.

He hovered over me again and started to stroke his cock before quickly ramming it inside my mouth, slamming so hard into my throat that I felt bile rise up.

"Don't you fucking vomit on Daddy's cock," he scolded as he pulled out of my mouth.

"I'm sorry, Daddy," I cried, the tears streaming down my cheeks from gagging.

There was a sharp slap to my cheek before he took both of his hands and started to squeeze around my neck. He was suddenly inside of me and started to fuck me roughly, pressing harder onto my throat. My eyes began to flutter shut and the next thing I knew, Michael's cum was dripping out of me and he was panting on the bed above me; I had passed out and he kept fucking me.

"You've been such a good girl. Let's clean you up and I'll feed you."

I still felt lightheaded as he untied me and helped me up. I wobbled to his bathroom knowing that something was terribly wrong; I knew this was *all* wrong. I knew he was abusing me, but I couldn't help myself—I needed to please Daddy now. And I vowed to myself that I would continue to please him until the day I died.

# Now

"Jacqueline Olsen?"

I answered my phone as I sat downstairs at the hostel with a couple of the other guests while they watched an action film on Netflix.

"Um, yes?" I responded.

It was an LA area code, so I answered, hoping it was a potential job offer.

"This is Lauren from Bon Appétit. We'd like to offer you the server position you interviewed for if you can start tonight."

I gasped. "Of course. I can start right now." I jumped up from the couch.

She laughed. "Great. We'll need you for the 4 to 10 p.m. shift. Come dressed in black pants and a crisp, white button up shirt. Comfortable black shoes."

"Okay, yes! I will be there!"

"Thanks. See you then." She hung up, and I squealed with excitement.

I ran up to my room to grab my purse and go shopping for new work clothes. I had four hours until I had to be there. As I walked back downstairs, I grabbed my phone and realized I had no one to share this good news with. Loneliness suddenly crept up through my chest, and I stopped in my tracks. *Don't feel sorry for yourself, Jackie. You can do this.* I was surprised at my inner monologue—she was nice to me for once. I continued on, taking the bus to West Hollywood to the Beverly Center; the restaurant was only a few blocks away, and I wanted to reacquaint myself with the area. I spent many of my teenage years stealing from the shops at the Beverly Center and sneaking cans of beer from the gas station across the street.

As I walked around H&M, I felt my phone vibrating in my back pocket. I pulled it out, and my heart dropped when I saw that Elliott was calling. *Fuck, I said some pretty revealing things to him the other night.* I had dodged two of his calls since then, and we had only texted briefly. I couldn't get myself involved with such a stable, nice, handsome man. Plus, I would never be able to trust him. But I couldn't just ghost him.

I hesitantly answered. "Hey!" I feigned confidence.

"Hey stranger. How are you doing?" His deep voice melted everything inside my body.

"I'm fine. I just got a job. I'm looking for some work clothes right now," I responded, nervously keeping my other hand busy as I searched through the racks.

"Congratulations! That's great news. May I ask where?" He seemed truly happy and interested in what I was saying.

*God damnit.* "Uh, yeah. I'll be serving at Bon Appétit," I answered hesitantly.

"Oh, the one off Melrose? I love that place." There was still a smile in his voice. "That's a great place to be working. I bet you'll get a lot of good tips."

His optimism was infectious. "Let's hope so." I shrugged to myself.

"Maybe I can take you out for a celebratory dinner? As friends," he clarified.

I bit my lip as I smiled and shook my head. "I can't. I start tonight."

There was a pause. "Okay. Maybe a brunch sometime this week?"

I had to give it to him—he was persistent. I secretly loved it.

"Yeah, maybe," I said flirtatiously.

There was another pause. "Please let me know if I'm bothering you. I already feel really weird about being friends with a beautiful twenty-eight-year-old."

*Me? Beautiful? Not anymore.* I suddenly felt horrible that he felt this way.

"No, no...you're not bothering me. I just...I really need to make it clear that I can't be in a relationship. Like, ever. I'm truly a fucking mess," I blurted out.

"I understand that. Just friends," he said, as if we were making a deal.

*Why do I still feel terrible?*

"And it's not that I don't find you attractive. You're...God, you're gorgeous. Too gorgeous. Like I said, I am just—"

"A mess," he interrupted, teasing me.

I let out a small laugh. "A mess."

"I appreciate your compliments. You're gorgeous as well. But you seem to be...much more than that," he admitted, almost sounding like he was surprised at himself for saying it.

"Nope. It's all just trauma under this layer of skin, I assure you." *And on top of my skin.*

He chuckled softly. "Okay. I believe you. I hope you have a really great first night. If you feel like it, let me know how it goes."

*I wish it were possible to go through this phone and give him a hug.* I was desperate for some sort of physical touch, but the last time I was that desperate, I ended up literally going crazy.

"I will. Thanks, Elliott," I said, smiling into the phone.

"Bye, Jacqueline."

His voice and the way he said my name continued to make my pussy pulse. *God, I'm fucked.*

"Bye," I breathed into the phone and quickly hung up.

* * *

My first night went extremely well. I made enough tips to last me another week at the hostel. The customers were friendly, the cooks, hosts, and fellow servers were extremely helpful and nice, and my confidence boosted 110% when I got hit on several times. *If they only knew what I looked like underneath these clothes.*

As I took the bus home, my mind immediately wandered to Elliott. I couldn't count how many times I had muttered "*Fuck it*" to myself while in LA. I opened Instagram and messaged him: **Hi. I think it's time we exchange numbers? Here's mine…**

He responded back quickly, this time through text message: **Hi, it's Elliott. How did your first night go?**

I couldn't help but smile whenever I thought about him.

**Elliott who?** I sent and laughed to myself.

**You know, the guy you keep trying to push away. The hot one.**

I smirked as I replied: **Oh, *THAT* Elliott. Hi Hot Elliott. My first night went really well.**

**I'm glad. Do you want to meet for a drink?**

Fuck. *Don't give in, don't give in, don't give in.* Fuck it again. I responded: **Sure, where do you suggest?** I groaned out loud, garnering stares from other passengers.

A few minutes passed before he responded again: **There's a cool place near me. I'll send you the address. Or I can pick you up if you'd like?**

My heartbeat whooshed in my ears as I replied: **Okay. You know where I am. See you in an hour?**

*Fuck fuck fuck fuck.*

I got back to the hostel and quickly changed into jeans and my usual scoop-neck, long-sleeved bodysuit—a staple to hide my scars—which I had in every color. I didn't have any time to think about what I was doing. I threw on a jacket and touched up my makeup just as I got his text: **I'm here.** I grabbed my purse and quickly headed down the stairs, almost falling over when I saw him standing in the lobby. I thought he'd be sitting in his car, waiting for me, but I should have known he'd be a gentleman. He wore a black henley that showcased his glorious muscles, paired with jeans and "Old Skool" Vans. I was pretty sure my jaw dropped to the floor as I approached him.

"Hi." I smiled. "Hot Elliott?" I teased.

He laughed and looked down at the floor—I was making him blush. *How is that possible?*

"That's what they call me." He shrugged, looking back up at me. "Shall we?" He gestured toward the door.

I nodded and followed him as he opened the door for me and walked us to his car parked down the street. Of course, he had a Prius; he probably recycled, gave money to charity, and fed stray cats in his neighborhood. He opened the passenger door for me and I kept repeating to myself: *Do not trust him. Just because he's nice doesn't mean he's not a monster.* He got into the driver's seat and started the car, glancing over at me with a smile before he drove off. I sensed that he was nervous. I couldn't figure out, for the life of me, why he'd be nervous around me.

"So, Jacqueline. Not to pry, but don't you have family around here you can stay with? Since you're from here?" he asked as we waited at a red light.

I sighed as I looked ahead. "I don't have family anymore," I answered vaguely.

"Oh, I'm sorry," he quickly apologized.

I shook my head as I turned to smile at him. "You didn't know. It would be safe to assume I have family here. But I was an only child and...I lost my parents when I was young." *Why am I volunteering this information?*

He quickly glanced over at me with sad eyes as he drove. "That's rough. My dad died when I was young too. I know how traumatizing that can be."

"I'm sorry." I wanted to change the subject. "So, where exactly do you live, Hot Elliott?" I asked, hoping to divert the attention to him.

He was smiling now.

"I'm in Los Feliz, not very far from here."

I nodded. I only knew of beautiful houses and good dive bars in Los Feliz.

"And why exactly are you single?" I wanted to get the hard-hitting questions out of the way.

He looked over at me with a surprised grin that quickly faded. "If you must know—I'm widowed. I lost my wife four years ago."

My heart dropped. *Oh no.* "I'm...I'm so sorry." I shook my head at myself. *Okay, so maybe he's perfect...and maybe he really is just a nice guy.* My guard was starting to slowly fall to the ground.

## NOW

He shook his head as well. "Yeah. So...you're really the first woman I've talked to for this long since she passed."

My mouth shot wide open. "Why *me*?" I muttered.

He took a moment to respond as we pulled into a parking lot that looked familiar; I realized it was across the street from a grocery store I used to frequent.

His face grew even more serious. "I don't know. I just felt... drawn to you for some reason. I can't really explain it." He shook his head at himself and I wanted to reach over and kiss him. Instead, I made a self-deprecating joke.

"Because you're a therapist and can sense a crazy person when you see one." I laughed.

He gave me a small smile as he turned to me. "You keep calling yourself crazy—a mess. I'm not sure if a 'crazy mess' could be in Los Angeles for just a few days and land a great job like you have. You're completely self-aware, maybe even painfully so, and that must be hard for someone who seems so sensitive and smart."

I nodded, tears forming in my eyes.

"I'm sorry. I didn't mean to upset you," he said with widened eyes.

I laughed, a coping mechanism for any strong feeling. "It's okay. I'm sure you're aware that I make self-deprecating jokes to mask how I really feel. As a therapist, I'm sure you can see right through me." I shrugged.

He shook his head. "This isn't from a therapist's perspective. It's from...me. I know you're really smart and kind—I can tell that. And funny." He raised his eyebrows at me playfully. "You've told me about your trauma and how you can't trust anyone. But I think...I think it's okay to let your guard down sometimes."

I stared at him, my eyes falling to his lips. My guard was still up and fully locked. *Does he always use these lines on women he meets? How do I know he hasn't said this to a million other women before me?*

"I...I can never trust anyone, Elliott. You don't understand the extent of my trauma. It's amazing that I even agreed to come have a drink with you," I admitted, tears pooling in my eyes again.

He nodded. "I'm sorry for upsetting you. Do you think we can still try to have a nice night? Or would you like me to take you back home?" He seemed upset with himself. He wasn't trying to be pushy, he wasn't trying to kiss me; he was just *talking* to me. And he was offering me an out.

I sighed then smiled. "I really want to have this drink with you. I think that's what terrifies me the most."

His lips slowly curled into a smile. "If at any time I make you uncomfortable, please don't hesitate to tell me. Or you can just tell me to fuck off. Then I'll get you an Uber home."

I shook my head. "Oh, you sweet thing. By the end of the night, I'm sure I'll have made you more uncomfortable than you've ever felt." I was warning him now; I knew I would probably say too much with some drinks in me.

He laughed and nodded. "We'll see."

# Then

I endured more abuse from Michael, but I welcomed it—it meant that he paid attention to me. All that I wanted was for him to keep telling me that I was his, and he continued to do so. He would hurt me in some way or another during sex and I would come for him, then he'd come inside of me. I never spent any time with him outside of sex and the aftercare he'd provide, ensuring I remained obsessed with him after he hurt me, stringing me along. He even said that to me while he bathed me one night after using all of my holes for his pleasure.

"One day, you're not going to be as obsessed with me as you are now. It will be over, and you won't want to be mine anymore."

I gasped as I looked up at him sitting at the edge of the tub.

"That will never happen, Daddy. I will love you until the day I die," I said with tears already flowing down my cheeks, dripping into the bath water.

"No. You will tire of me. It always happens." He shook his head at me knowingly.

I was getting upset now. "It's not going to happen with me. I love you more than anything, Daddy."

Now his jaw was clenching. "You don't know what love is, Jackie. You're just a little girl who hangs onto my every word.

You don't even know me."

I began to tremble. Why was he being so cruel?

"Are you trying to get rid of me?" I asked with frustration.

He looked down at me with absolutely nothing in his eyes. "If I wanted you gone, you'd be gone."

I somehow found that comforting; *I'm still here—I'm still his.*

"Why can't I stay with you? Just for one night?" I was desperate to be in his presence, even when he was spiteful.

He smiled as he pulled the plug from the drain. He liked my desperation. "Those are the rules, baby."

I stood up as he took a towel and wrapped it around my body. "Can't we break the rules for just one night?" My whiny voice was repulsive.

"No. The rules are there for a reason," he said, running his finger gently across my collarbone. "And once they're broken, nothing will ever be the same."

# Now

Elliott turned the head of every woman as we walked into the bar, searching for a spot to sit. It was packed, and the music was loud, but I liked the relaxed and friendly atmosphere.

"What am I getting you?" Elliott leaned in to ask, and I could smell his clean, crisp cologne.

"Vodka seven. Thank you," I responded in his ear.

He ordered our drinks, then looked over at me and smiled. "I'm sorry, I didn't know it would be so loud. I've actually never been here, but I drive past it every day." He had to lean into me again to speak. It was going to drive me crazy if he kept getting so close to me.

I shook my head at him teasingly.

"It's fine. It looks like there's a patio outside. Should we move out there?" I nodded toward the door leading outside.

He looked over, then back at me. "Let's do it."

Once we got our drinks, I followed him out to the patio, where only a few others sat. It was mid-January, and anything under 60 degrees was considered freezing in LA, so most people were inside.

We sat facing each other at a small, round table, and I was suddenly nervous; this felt like a date.

"So, Jacqueline," Elliott started, obviously nervous as he

took a deep breath.

I chugged down half of my drink. I needed liquid courage. "Elliott," I responded, just as nervously.

"Do you know, uh…are you planning on staying where you're at now? In that neighborhood?" He took a small sip of his drink.

I shrugged. "I think so. I like the area. I used to live in Burbank and the valley when…I lived here," I trailed off, suddenly realizing I was opening up that topic.

He nodded. "I've been around Burbank as well. My office is actually over there," he explained.

*Okay, let's put the focus back on him.* "How long have you been a therapist?" I took another big sip of my drink.

"Um…about ten years now. Have you been in the restaurant business for long?" He shifted in his seat, eagerly waiting for my response.

"My entire adult life." I smiled. "Actually…I lived in Vegas for two years and…" I trailed off, unsure why I was about to tell him about that time in my life. *Am I testing him? Or am I just tipsy already?*

He raised his eyebrows, waiting for me to continue.

"I was a stripper. That was my first job," I went on.

He blinked and gave me a grin, showing off his perfect teeth. "Well, I wasn't expecting to hear that."

"I wasn't expecting to tell you." I laughed, my cheeks burning.

"Did you also do that in New York?" he asked curiously.

I shook my head. "No. That's where I started in the restaurant business."

He nodded, watching me intently before he slowly smiled.

"What?" I grew even more nervous.

## NOW

"You're just so full of surprises."

He tilted his head as he looked at me, observing me like I was the Mona Lisa.

I wanted to tell him how much I liked him. I wanted to tell him that he already made me so happy. But I couldn't—I could never let myself fall in love again.

I slammed down the rest of my vodka seven. "I need another drink."

He stood up quickly. "Let me get it for you."

He was halfway to the door before I jumped out of my seat and followed him. *Trust no one. He could be putting roofies in my drink.* "I'll come with you."

We came back outside with my second drink while Elliott still nursed his first.

"So, can I ask you what made you come back to LA?" he asked as we sat back down.

I sighed heavily. "Um...let's just say a bad breakup. A really bad breakup," I answered vaguely. "It happened four years ago."

He raised his eyebrows. "That's a good enough reason." He nodded, finally taking a sip of his drink. "You still haven't made me uncomfortable yet, by the way." He smiled, and I felt my heart flipping around, begging me to run, to save him from me eventually ruining everything.

"Do you want to know why I'm traumatized?" I dared him, taking another big swig of my drink.

He eyed my drink and nodded. "If you're comfortable with telling me. You're not obligated to tell me anything you don't want to."

*Is he actually perfect? Fuck.*

"My dad killed my mom when I was six, and I'm the one who

found her. A man that I had a...relationship with tied me up and mutilated my body. He continued to do so for months. He's in prison, but he just called me before I decided to move here. He was trying to scare me, and it worked. Now I know I will never be able to trust another man again because every fucking man I've ever loved has destroyed me and my life."

I was crying. *Great.* Elliott's face never showed any emotion until he started speaking.

"Jacqueline." He shook his head, his eyes full of sorrow. "I'm so sorry you had to go through that. I don't even know what to say except that I can't imagine what you're possibly feeling. And...now I understand why you're so wary of me." He cleared his throat and put his hand on the table, as if he wanted to reach out to me. "I have no intention of hurting you, even as your friend."

My lips twitched into a smile.

"Well, you're easily the best therapist I've ever talked to." I laughed. "And the most attractive." I couldn't believe the words coming out of my mouth; I was tipsy, but not *that* tipsy. And I had just told him my whole life story, and he didn't even fucking flinch.

He looked down at the table and smiled, obviously blushing.

"Have I made you uncomfortable enough yet?" I teased.

"Believe it or not, no."

I couldn't deny it anymore—I was starting to fall for him. I needed to run, but my feet were firmly planted on the ground, pointed towards him, and I had no intention of ever turning them.

# Then

I started to make excuses for not being able to see Michael. I didn't know if he believed them or not. I was starting to realize that he didn't love me the way I loved him. Even in my deranged love for him, I knew I was being treated poorly. Fuck, worse than poorly—he was abusing me. I could only give so much; I gave him my heart, my body, my dignity. And he was right: I didn't know anything about him. I started questioning why I loved him so much. I started questioning why he even wanted me around. He continued to pay for the things I needed like rent and food, but I wondered if he did those things because he cared about me or because he just wanted me to rely on him.

I had planned on breaking things off when I went to his apartment, thinking it would be the last time I ever saw him. It was killing me, but I needed to leave before things got worse. When we first started our relationship, he told me I would always have the option to leave. Was that still true?

He answered the door with a smile on his face; I thought it was odd—he never greeted me that way. "There you are, my sweet girl."

He took my hand and pulled me inside, and I realized he had been drinking—I could smell it on him.

He sat on the couch and outstretched his hand to me. "Sweet

Jackie, come sit on Daddy's lap."

*If I do that, I will never be able to break things off.*

"Actually, Daddy—Michael." I stood there feebly as my hands trembled.

I could already see the anger blazing in his eyes.

"I don't..." I looked to the ground. "I don't think we can see each other anymore."

I finally looked up at him when he didn't respond. His jaw was clenching, and he stared at the floor in front of my feet.

"Please. Don't leave. Stay with me tonight. I will take care of you."

I was startled by his gentle tone. He looked up at me with soft, caring eyes—something I had never seen from him before.

My heart ached. This was exactly what I wanted; I wanted him to show me that he cared.

"Really?" Tears pooled in my eyes.

He outstretched his hand to me again. "Yes, baby. Come."

I slowly walked to him and grabbed his hand; he was so warm and gentle. He smiled and patted on his lap. I carefully sat down on him and instantly felt the erection under my thighs. I was already wet; it was a guarantee whenever he touched me. He pulled my waist and positioned me directly on top of his hard cock with my back to his chest.

He had one arm held around my waist while his other hand crept up my shirt. I knew he could feel the banging in my chest as he pushed his hand under my bra and began to tease my nipple.

"Daddy could never let you leave, baby," he said quietly into my ear, his warm breath sent tingles throughout my body.

I closed my eyes, already hypnotized by his touch. He had never touched me so sensually, so carefully before.

"Why do you want to leave, hm?" he went on, moving to my other breast.

"I...I want you to love me," I whispered, the tears already trailing down my cheeks.

He chuckled softly. "Oh baby, Daddy does love you. Don't you know that?" He pressed his lips to my neck.

I let out an involuntary moan.

"I love you, Daddy," I breathed, starting to grind my hips against his erection.

His hand quickly grazed up my chest, then closed tightly around my neck. He began to squeeze as he locked both of my arms behind my back, rendering me defenseless. I tried to kick my feet against the floor but he was too strong. *I'm going to die. He's finally going to kill me.*

"Then don't you ever try to leave me again. If you do, I will kill you, Jackie," he snarled into my ear, finally releasing his grip on my neck and leaving me gasping for air.

I began to cry as he continued to hold my arms behind my back.

"Get on your knees. You need to be punished for trying to leave." He pushed me away and I fell to the floor, still catching my breath.

I cried on all fours, leaving my head hanging. "I'm sorry, Daddy."

*Why did I think I could leave? Does he actually love me or did he just need to hear that I still loved him?*

There was suddenly a sharp blow to my ass.

"Your knees, Jackie. Don't make me say it again!" he yelled.

I quickly got to my knees as I faced him, too scared to look him in the eye. I was even too scared to continue to cry. He was already pulling down his jeans as I stared down at the floor, waiting for whatever he was going to do to me.

"First, you're going to suck my cock until I come all over you. Then I'm going to make sure no man could ever want you again." He pulled his cock out and I started to cry again. "You're all mine, Jackie. And I will make sure you never forget it."

# Now

Elliott drove me home that night, opened the car door for me, and walked me into the lobby—all the gentlemanly things a man could do. He didn't try to kiss me or even hug me. I started to think that maybe he really did want to *only* be my friend. Or was he really just that respectful?

I hated that I didn't have privacy to masturbate in my own room, so I took the opportunity to use the shower in the empty bathroom. I closed my eyes, lathering my body with soap, and imagined Elliott in his car, reaching his hand over and in between my thighs. Fuck, just *thinking* about him made me wet; I slipped my hand to my pussy and put my finger to my throbbing clit, needing release after being in his presence and not being able to touch him. *Why do I have these rules again?* My mind instantly wandered to Michael and I hated that his face began to mix with Elliott's in my fantasy.

"Elliott," I whispered to myself, hoping his name said aloud would rule out the image of Michael.

Elliott slid his finger inside of me, feeling the heat and wetness between my thighs. He put his fingers to his mouth to taste me and—

"Fuck," I quietly moaned, coming to my own fantasy.

This was exactly why I needed to run; I was starting to let my guard down with him *and* I wanted nothing more than for him to fuck me. I told him about Michael mutilating me because I wanted to scare him off. But was that really all I was trying to do? Was I giving him a warning? Or was I opening up and telling him things that he needed to know before we—before we what? Started a relationship? I knew that could never happen so why exactly was I opening up to him? Why was I even spending time with him?

I knew what I needed to do—I needed to get him out of my life. I needed to keep myself safe. That meant staying far away from any man, friendly and otherworldly beautiful or not.

I decided to sleep on my decision. When I woke up from a dream in which Elliott and I had a picnic and had sex during sunset, I knew I had to cut things off with him.

I was on my way to work when I sent him the text: **I had such a nice time with you last night. That's why it's so hard to let you know that we can't talk anymore. I am letting every one of my guards down with you and I'm not comfortable with how that's making me feel. I hope you understand. You're far too good to be in my life. 💔**

*Fuck!* I accidentally hit send without erasing the broken heart emoji. I turned my phone off and silently cried the rest of the way to work.

\* \* \*

I was on my break when I decided to turn my phone back on. I had been having a decent night with decent tips but my mind was constantly on Elliott. My heart dropped when I saw that I had three texts from him queued up on my phone.

The first one read: **I understand. I'm sorry you're not com-**

fortable. **Like I said, I don't want you to feel uncomfortable in any way around me.** The next one read: **If we're not going to talk anymore, I guess I'd like to get a few things off my chest in case I never get to talk to you again.** I knew I was going to cry, whatever he had to tell me.

His last one read: **You have stirred up feelings inside of me that I didn't even know were possible anymore. I was instantly drawn to you, even when you continually told me to—for a lack of a better term—fuck off. I was excited about our friendship even though I knew I wanted more; I just wanted to talk to you, if that's all I could do. I was not looking for anyone at all when you begrudgingly accepted my help on that plane, but now I know that I don't want just anyone, I want you.**

I read his last text over and over, my heart pounding harder each time. Thoughts couldn't even form in my brain—all I could see were the words "I want you" at the end of his text. My hands were shaking as I tried to respond, but there was nothing I could say. I wanted him so fucking badly, and I couldn't have him. *Why can't you have him, you idiot? Because I'm fucked up! Once he knows you, who you really are, he will just end up hurting you. Just give him the chance. No. I can't.*

I spent my whole break trying to think of what to say to him. In the end, I pocketed my phone and returned to work, my mind flying away, far out of my head.

By the time I got off work, I quickly texted him before I could change my mind: **What's your address?**

He instantly texted me back. I ordered an Uber, and twenty minutes later, I was pulling up to his house on a hill in Los Feliz. It looked smaller than I imagined, but I figured it must have cost more than a million dollars. *God, I am way out of my league here.* I walked up the steps and didn't even have to knock; Elliott opened the door as soon as I approached. He looked nervous in his jeans and T-shirt, his arms even more muscular than they had seemed under his long-sleeved shirts.

"Hi," I breathed, my heart viciously trying to break out of my chest.

He eyed me as I walked up, my legs feeling wobbly as I stood directly in front of him. "Hi."

"I shouldn't be here," my shaky voice let out.

"I'm glad that you are," he responded, searching my face, his chest moving up and down quickly.

*Fuck it.* I quickly pressed my body against his as I reached up for his shoulders, his lips finding mine in an instant. He held onto me with his strong arms around my waist, pressing me even closer to him. His tongue urgently twirled with mine as he guided us into the house, quickly closing the door behind us with his foot. My hands had a mind of their own as they, with his help, lifted his shirt up and over his head and I moaned as I felt his hard body underneath my fingers. I unlocked our kiss to look at his body—*fucking hell, oh my God.* My breath hitched as I stared at him; he had a sexy, manly hairy chest, and his arms were bulky like fucking Thor.

"I have rules," I breathed. "My shirt stays on." I was too self-conscious to show him my scars; the ones on my legs weren't nearly as bad as those on my upper half.

"Jacqueline, we don't have to do this—"

I shut him up as I pressed my mouth against his, my hands finding the button to his jeans and quickly unzipping him, reaching for the erection I felt when his body was pressed against mine. I gasped when I felt him; he was huge and thick and I wondered if my body would be able to take him.

Elliott started to unbutton my pants and quickly slid them down, feeling around my bare ass that my thong exposed. I was dripping wet as I tugged his boxer briefs down and felt his warm, hard cock under my palm. I pulled away from our kiss to look down at him and I immediately got to my knees, desperately needing to have him in my mouth.

"Fuck, your cock is the best thing I've ever seen," I said as I looked up at him, then opened my mouth wide to take him in.

I could only wrap my lips around the head of his cock; he was too fucking big for anything else. I moved my hands up and down his shaft while my tongue followed, searching his eyes as I did so. He looked down at me, his eyes coated with desire, holding my hair back gently with one hand and the other hand tracing my lip with his thumb. I kept looking between his god-like abs and his lustful eyes. His tongue traced his bottom lip as he stared down at me, his eyebrows pulled together in concentration.

"Come here," he said before he took my hand and lifted me to my feet, guiding me to the couch behind us.

He sat me down and slowly removed my thong, throwing them over his shoulder before spreading open my thighs and getting to his knees. I watched his muscled arms contract as he took my legs and put them over his shoulders, eyeing my pussy hungrily before pressing his mouth to it.

"Holy fucking shit," I breathed as he buried his tongue inside of me, his nose practically rubbing my clit as he looked up at me with a smile.

He quickly removed his face as he stared up at me. "Come on my face, Jacqueline. I want to make you come until your legs tremble on my shoulders." He buried his face into me again and swirled his tongue against my clit, the pleasure so intense that it made me come instantly. I felt the vibration of his moan on me, forcing another orgasm and only giving me a few seconds before the build of another, then another.

"Please," I cried. "I need you inside of me, Elliott."

He lifted his head up and quickly hovered over me, pressing his mouth to mine, the taste of myself on his lips turning me on even more. He was suddenly lifting me up with his arms underneath my knees as I held onto his shoulders. His eyes never left mine as he stood up, his gaze unwavering and intense, and easily thrust inside of me, jerking his hips up and bouncing me on his cock.

"Oh my God!" I moaned loudly, his cock perfectly hitting my g-spot, a fierce orgasm building.

"Fuck, you take my cock so well," he grunted, seemingly not even breaking a sweat as he continued to bounce me up and down.

His dirty talk instantly had my pussy seizing and making me come; I didn't even have time to think before he laid me back down on the couch and lifted my legs to his chest, quickly pushing his cock into me and furiously pounding.

"Tell me if you can't take it, baby," he exhaled, holding my calves as he stared down at me.

"Your cock is fucking perfect." I smiled, pushing my hips against him as he continued to pound me.

"You keep talking like that and you're gonna make me come, baby." He grinned, clenching onto my legs tighter.

"As long as you let me taste it," I quickly responded, putting my hands up to his arms.

He grunted as he pounded me harder before he lifted me up, his cock still inside me, and sat on the couch as I straddled him.

"I need to make you come more. Seeing you come fucking

## NOW

turns me on more than anything," he said as he took my hips and started to grind me against him.

I paused, unsure of myself. I hadn't been on top in...many, many years. I was never able to do anything remotely like this with...*him*. Did I still even know how to get off like this?

He could sense my hesitation. "What's wrong?"

"I just...I haven't been in this position in a really long time," I admitted. "Do you think I can make you come like this?"

He smiled and put his big hands to my cheeks. "It doesn't matter if you make *me* come, baby. Your pleasure is all that matters."

My heart dropped to my pussy. I immediately began to grind on him, moving my hips up and down, our eye contact never breaking. He took my ass with his hands and helped me grind up and down on his length, my orgasm quickly approaching.

"Come on, baby. Come on my cock," he ordered, and his words spiraled me into an intense orgasm, my body quivering as I chased the pleasure that felt better than anything I'd ever felt.

He waited until I slowed my hips to kiss me fervently, then lifted me off his cock and pushed me down onto the floor on my knees. He took his cock in his hand and began to stroke, his other hand gently holding onto the back of my head.

"Come in my mouth. Please," I begged, bouncing on my knees, my nipples hardened at the sight of him masturbating.

He suddenly pushed my head down to his cock and grunted loudly, spurts shooting into my mouth, his warm and salty cum pooling there as I waited for his last drop. He watched me as I opened my mouth to show him and I smiled as I swallowed, then opened my mouth to display it.

"Jesus Christ, Jacqueline." He leaned down and lifted me up, my wet pussy sliding against his cock, as he began to urgently kiss me again.

I giggled as we parted, unable to contain my excitement; I couldn't remember the last time I *giggled*. I almost didn't realize that my button up shirt had opened and started to reveal the hideous white scars on my stomach until Elliott quickly glanced down at my breasts. I hurriedly buttoned up the bottom, leaving my breasts on display.

"You don't have to hide them from me, Jacqueline. I think you're so God damn beautiful, inside and out." He was so earnest and sweet even after he just came into my mouth.

I tried to hide my smile as I looked down at his perfect chest and abs, suddenly feeling embarrassed.

"Yeah, well, your opinion might change once this shirt is off." I sighed as I stood up and grabbed my underwear.

I knew that when I turned to face him, he would see Michael's name carved on the top of my thighs, if he hadn't already. I suddenly felt Elliott's hands on my shoulders, his soft lips pressed to the side of my neck. I turned around to look up at him, almost too distracted by his body and semi-hard cock pressing against me.

His eyes boring into mine made my knees weak.

"Elliott...if this is going to work, I have a lot to tell you."

# Then

I passed out after he carved the first few letters into my skin.

I had been tied to his bed, kicking and screaming while he did so, before he placed duct tape over my mouth to shut me up. I was stripped naked and watched as he pulled a sharp knife out, holding it up beside his face.

"You never should have tried to leave me, little girl," he growled, his eyes bloodshot red, I assumed from his drunkenness.

My heart pounded in my chest, my limbs too exhausted from straining against the rope tied to my ankles and wrists.

"Now you won't be able to. You will have my name carved all over your weak, pathetic body. You will be too ashamed to show any other man your hideous scars. Won't you?"

I began to cry. It was pointless to do anything else at that point. I wasn't sure if I even wanted to live anymore; I think I wanted him to hurt me beyond repair at that point.

He walked towards me and quickly jumped on top of me, straddling me between his legs. I saw his erection clear underneath his jeans—he was getting off on this.

"I don't think my name will suffice. Perhaps I should write 'slut' as well? I mean, that's what you are for trying to leave me."

Then he began to cut into my stomach. The pain seared through my body, the stinging on my skin worse than any blow he could give me.

"S." He was smiling, slowly gliding the knife across my skin. "L." My eyes began to flutter shut. "U."

I was too scared to even move...and then, with the pain unbearable, I passed out.

I woke up still tied to the bed, my whole body on fire. Michael was nowhere to be seen. I looked down at my body and saw blood oozing from the wounds on my stomach and thighs. I began to sob, afraid of Michael coming back and doing more damage to me. After my tears were all dried out, I realized the sun was starting to come up. I heard movement outside the bedroom; I shut my eyes tight to avoid seeing Michael walk through the door. The door creaked open and I began to shake. I could hear his footsteps inching closer to the bed as he sighed.

"It really is a shame, my sweet girl. I didn't want to hurt you like this. But you never should have tried to leave me." His voice was almost a whisper.

I opened my eyes, tears falling down the sides of my cheeks.

"Oh, baby. Don't cry. You're bound to me for life, doesn't that excite you?"

I froze. *Bound to him?*

"Look, I even got you a ring." He smiled as he sat down beside me, holding up a silver band. "It's for my sweet girl. Inside it's engraved 'Daddy's girl.'" He slipped the ring on my left ring finger.

My brain instantly went from hatred back to obsession. *He cares about me. He loves me. He bought me a ring.*

"Do you love it, baby?" He looked up at me as he grazed my breast softly with his hand.

I nodded slowly.

"Let me untie you. Let's get you cleaned up and I will take care of these wounds for you."

The burning on my skin started to subside. Now it was set in stone: I could never leave him. I was always going to belong to him. I was bound to him forever, and somehow...I was okay with that.

# Now

Elliott led me down the hall into his bedroom after he put on his boxer briefs, much to my dismay. We passed a picture in the hall of a beautiful, strawberry blonde woman that almost looked like a headshot. *Was his wife an actress? How did she pass?* I had so many questions for him, but first, I needed to tell him about my life.

The first thing I noticed about his bedroom was the abstract art above his bed. The bed was neatly made on an iron rod frame, with nightstands on either side. Books were stacked next to a lamp on one side, while the other table was bare apart from the lamp.

"Are you comfortable talking in here? Or would you like to go back out to the living room?" He stood next to the bed, his eyes full of concern.

*Still such a gentleman even after fucking me senseless.* I'm sure he was nervous to hear all about my trauma.

"Here is fine." I crossed my arms as I sat down with him on the bed.

I was self-conscious all over again; that was easily the best sex I had ever had, with the best-looking man, and now I had to tell him all about how fucked up I was.

He scooted back and lifted the covers, patting the bed next

## NOW

to him with a grin. I blushed as I crawled onto the bed and got under the covers with him. He put his arm out on my pillow, and as I lay my head down, I realized he wanted to cuddle. I felt like sobbing—*is this the real deal?* He wanted to cuddle with me and hold me while I told him my deepest, darkest secrets?

I put my arm over his chest, running my fingers through the hair that covered it. He pulled me closer, and I felt his lips press against the top of my head.

"I have to tell you, I'm not used to this. I was never allowed to...do this in my previous relationship," I started quietly.

"No? Why not?" His deep voice was calm and soothing.

*Am I really going to volunteer this information?*

"You know how I told you how I was tied up and mutilated?" *As if he would forget.*

"Yes." I heard his heart pounding in his chest.

My heart sank. *Why am I telling him this? He's gonna run, Jackie. Don't do this.*

"I agreed to be tied up. I...I consented to it most of the time," I began. "Obviously I didn't consent to getting his fucking name and other horrible things carved onto my body. But...we had a dominant/submissive relationship. At least that's what he called it. And a severely deranged one at that."

I waited for him to react; I was glad that I couldn't see the look on his face as I buried my face into his chest.

"Please go on. I'm listening," he finally said, gently rubbing the tips of his fingers up and down my covered arms.

"We met on a BDSM app. I was instantly obsessed with him, and he was instantly horrible to me. I had never been a submissive before, but I was curious. He raped me the first night we met, but I thought because he made me come that it was okay. He acted as if he did nothing wrong. Then he told me that I was *his*. And that sparked something inside of me because all I had ever wanted was for someone to just *want* me."

My tears were falling onto his chest.

"He became more and more abusive. I tried to leave him and then he...he..." I began to sob, unable to continue as my shoulders heaved into Elliott's arms.

He put both arms around me and held me until my crying slowed several minutes later.

"Jacqueline, you know that's not what a dominant/submissive relationship is supposed to be like. Right?" His voice was careful and gentle.

My eyebrows pulled together with confusion. Of course I knew that. But surely he didn't have any experience with that, did he?

I finally looked up at him, his strong jaw clenching as he looked down at me. His eyes were still soft but I could tell he was upset.

"Yes, I know that now. Is that something...you're familiar with?" I held my breath—I didn't even know what I wanted his answer to be.

He blinked before he answered, never pulling his gaze from mine. "Yes. My wife and I...we explored a lot of that during our marriage."

My jaw would have dropped if it wasn't resting on his chest. "How so?" I asked eagerly.

"Well, Kate came to me with it. My wife—her name was Kate," he said, and I smiled. "We had been married for a couple of years when she told me she wanted to try something new; she wanted to be dominated. So I did my research, we tried some things out, and I found myself enjoying being a dom. I liked a mixture of things—being a traditional dom, a pleasure dom, a rigger."

I started to get aroused again. His words from earlier during sex stuck out immediately: seeing me come turned him on more than anything and my pleasure was all that mattered.

He smiled as he added, "I am also very into primal play. The list could go on."

"I don't even know what any of that means." I laughed, embarrassed. "All I know is that I enjoy being told what to do."

Elliott smiled at me again, seemingly holding something back.

"What?" I smirked, getting up on my elbow.

"I could tell during sex that you were submissive. Begging for my cock, asking me with a 'please.'" He almost looked embarrassed to be talking to me this way.

I looked down at my empty left-hand ring finger.

"Do you like to be called anything in particular while you're being dominant?" I looked up at him hesitantly.

He gave me a soft smile. "Before we get into this, I'd still like to get to know each other better, if you're okay with that."

*I think I'm in love.* I nodded and slowly sat up, unbuttoning my shirt. Somehow, I was ready to show him. The fear that had always held me back seemed to dissipate in his presence. My heart pounded in my chest, but there was a strange sense of calm washing over me. I took a deep breath, feeling the weight of my past and the scars that marked my body, both seen and unseen. In this moment, I knew that showing him meant revealing not just my physical vulnerabilities, but also the emotional wounds that haunted me for so long. Yet, with him, I felt a glimmer of hope that maybe, just maybe, he would understand and accept all of me.

"You don't have to—"

"I *want* to," I interrupted. "I don't want to be ashamed with you."

I let my shirt fall off my shoulders, down onto the bed, and removed the blanket from my lower half. I watched his jaw clench and his eyebrows pull together slightly as his eyes scanned my body. I looked down at the "Michael's Property" scar on my stomach, then to his name on one arm and his name plus "slut" on the other. My upper thighs bore the same marks on each leg.

"Besides the physical pain he inflicted, the emotional scars he left may be even worse."

"He's in prison? Because if not, I'm going to kill him," he said quietly, his voice trembling with barely suppressed rage as he continued to eye my scars, his jaw clenched and his eyes burning with fury.

I realized he was dead serious.

"Yes, I think so, but he's getting out soon. He may be out already. I changed my number so he can't reach me anymore," I explained.

He sat up and sighed. "That's his name? Michael?" he asked, looking over at me, his face still serious, a mix of concern and anger etched in his features.

I laughed, the idea of Elliott hurting *anyone* bizarre to me, but his face never softened.

"Elliott, he doesn't matter anymore. He's out of my life." I shook my head and wrapped my arms around his shoulders, trying to reassure him.

He took a moment to respond, his head hanging low. "Thinking of anyone hurting you makes me..." he trailed off.

I pressed my mouth gently on his cheek, the light stubble

tickling my lips. "Let's talk about something else."

He nodded. "Okay," he whispered.

"What was your wife like? Is that okay to talk about?" I asked, sitting down next to him and putting my hand on his muscular thigh. I wondered when I would get over how hot he was.

Elliott looked over at me and smiled. "Yeah, I don't mind." He paused for a moment and linked his fingers with mine. "We were married for fourteen years. We bought this house together. She was an actress." His eyes lit up as he looked at me. "She was very kind and she loved art. She did this piece here." He gestured to the painting above his bed.

I eyed it with admiration. "It's beautiful. I love it."

He was quiet again before he spoke, his eyes on the floor. "She, um... she had cancer—pancreatic cancer. She died a year after the diagnosis."

My heart dropped. I immediately began to tear up. Why was *I* crying? "Fuck, I'm so sorry." I shook my head. He immediately looked over at me and gave me a sad smile.

"She had your dirty mouth too," he said, eyeing me fondly.

Every time he looked at me like that, my heart grew wider and softer. He tucked a strand of hair behind my ear and surveyed my face.

"Is it too soon to ask you to stay the night? I haven't done this in...almost twenty years." He grinned, almost looking embarrassed.

Holy shit; I kept forgetting he was eighteen years older than me. And the fact that he wanted me to stay the night meant more to me than the sex. Of course, the sex was amazing, but I wanted connection. I wanted to be wanted.

"I would love to stay the night," I replied.

We cuddled in bed, my first time actually intimately cuddling, and I fell asleep in his arms knowing that deep down, obsessive Jackie was on the horizon.

# Then

Something in me changed when Michael cut and scarred my body. I hated him but I loved him. I never wanted to be without him but I didn't want to stay. I wanted to please him but I wanted him to fuck off.

He knew he had me right where he wanted me. He made it so I could never leave him, even if he left me. He wanted me bound to him only for his benefit. I had nothing on him. He could literally push me to the curb, and I would have nothing to fight with, nothing to show for.

The abuse continued, but I begged to stay with him every night. I could tell he was getting tired of me. I could see him rolling his eyes, somehow bored while I sat on my knees with his cock in my mouth. I knew he was going to stop caring about me soon, and I didn't know how to keep him. I was desperate for him to just fucking love me. I was desperate for his undivided attention.

I don't know why I thought trying to kill myself would suddenly make him realize that he was in love with me. But after one of our sessions, after he cleaned me in the bath and while I was supposed to get dressed, I decided to go into his kitchen drawer and find the sharpest knife I could find. I waited until he finished in the bathroom and came walking into the kitchen.

He scolded me right away as I held the knife to my wrist. "Jackie!"

"I don't want to live if you don't love me," I cried, pressing the knife to my skin.

"Don't be so fucking dramatic. Put the knife down. Now!" He was angry and inching closer to me.

*Do it, Jackie! Make him love you or die.*

I quickly sliced the knife down my wrist and blood immediately started pouring out. He lunged toward me and grabbed a kitchen towel, pressing it against my wound as I fell to my knees and slumped back against the cabinet.

*He doesn't want me to die.*

"You fucking idiot, Jackie!"

I started getting lightheaded as I heard him yelling something. My eyes began fluttering shut as his voice became clearer: "She's losing a lot of blood. But I think she's dangerous—I'm going to need the police here as well."

# Now

I had never slept so well in my life. As soon as my eyes opened, my lips quickly twitched into a smile. Being in Elliott's arms gave me a sense of comfort, of feeling safe and wanted. I was able to stare freely at him while he slept, feeling like a creep but unable to help myself. His strong jawline, his full lips, his amazing body that sent a tingle straight to my pussy when I scanned my eyes over him. He had to have something wrong with him. Michael was the most beautiful thing I'd ever seen before Elliott, and look how he turned out. Someone like him could ruin me all over again. And would I stop him? My therapist in New York told me that it was okay to trust someone again, that not every man would be like Michael. But I was too scared to even try it before now. I wanted to lay out all the cards for Elliott and let him know what he'd be getting into. Better for him to leave now than when I was truly 100% in love with him.

"Good morning, Jacqueline." His hoarse morning voice took me out of my spiraling thoughts.

I looked up at him and realized I had been staring at his cock that was covered by only a thin sheet. *Real fucking smooth, Jackie.*

"Good morning." I smiled up at him.

"Did you sleep well?" He was running his fingertips up and down my bare arm; it felt so foreign to have someone touch me, especially there.

I nodded. "I did." I nuzzled my face back into his chest, never wanting to leave.

He ran his hand through my hair as if we had done this a million times before. My heart was already breaking because I knew this was too good to be true.

"Elliott, I have more to tell you." I looked up at him and saw his expectant eyes waiting for more of my sob story. "I mean, I don't *have* to tell you." I was starting to change my mind—I didn't want to lose him. I didn't want to burden him with my problems. He was too sweet and too good for my problems.

He nodded down at me. "I want to know."

I sighed heavily and sat up, covering myself with the sheets. "Maybe we should, like...have coffee first or something." I was stalling.

"Sure, if you'd like. How do you like it?" He was already standing up, waiting on my beck and call. I wasn't sure if I deserved it.

I laughed uneasily. "I'll help you." I started to stand up but realized I didn't have anything to wear; I wasn't ready to stand bare naked with him, revealing all of my scars in the morning light.

"Oh, let me get you something to put on." Elliott started for his dresser, already reading my mind, and I shamelessly checked him out in only his boxer briefs.

I watched him pull out a plain white T-shirt and bring it over to me. He smiled as he handed it to me. "Anything else? I'm afraid my joggers wouldn't fit you," he teased.

I took the T-shirt from him and shook my head. "We could

make it fit. We somehow did last night."

His eyebrows immediately lifted as he took in what I said. "Jacqueline," he teasingly scolded. "Do you always talk this dirty before breakfast?"

I shrugged and smiled as I pulled his shirt over my head. "You just bring it out of me."

He narrowed his eyes as he reached his hand out for me. "Come on, dirty girl. Let's get coffee before I pick you up and bounce you on my cock again."

My jaw dropped. *Holy shit.* I saw his cock hardening underneath the fabric of his boxer briefs.

I took his hand. "Well, keep talking to me that way and I'm gonna start begging for it."

He raised an eyebrow as he clasped his hand onto mine and guided me towards the kitchen. The natural light coming from the windows in the living room shone brightly and I realized his floor to ceiling front windows had no curtains or coverings. My mind quickly returned to the night before—had anyone seen us fucking in the living room? The idea turned me on more than I thought it would.

We walked into the kitchen, more natural light pouring in, and he began making coffee. I looked out the windows, noticing the trees surrounding the neighborhood made it feel like we were in a tropical escape rather than the heart of Los Angeles.

"I have sugar and creamer. There's some soy milk in here too," he explained, rummaging through his fridge.

"Just a little creamer is fine," I replied, still taking in his house.

I grabbed a chair from the small dining table and spotted a small deck on the side of the house.

"Your house is beautiful," I said, admiring the space as Elliott poured creamer into my mug.

"Thank you." He smiled and looked over at me. "I want to show you the backyard. There's a little deck out there. Let me get some clothes on, and we can head out."

He handed me my coffee and disappeared into his room. I continued exploring, peeking into the two other rooms from the hallway. One looked like an office, and the other was a guest room.

As I was glancing into the bathroom, Elliott emerged from his room in gray joggers (*is he doing this on purpose?*) and a black T-shirt, holding a blanket and his coffee.

"It's a bit chilly outside," he said, holding up the blanket and reaching for my hand.

I took his hand, and he led me out the back door. We descended wooden stairs to a paved walkway. His backyard was even greener than the front; trees lined each side, and a small hill sloped down to vibrant succulents and a lemon tree. At the end of the walkway stood a wooden deck with a pergola overhead and a small wooden table surrounded by comfortable chairs. As we approached, I noticed an outdoor loveseat with two small matching chairs beside it.

"This is one of my favorite places to be. It's so peaceful out here when everything else in the city feels so chaotic," he said, settling onto the loveseat and pulling me down with him.

He draped the blanket over us as I sat cross-legged, one knee resting lightly on his leg. A tingle ran through my belly when his hand brushed over the inside of my thigh.

"It's...it's beautiful out here," I murmured, almost too distracted by Elliott's touch.

We fell into silence for a moment, and I closed my eyes, listening to the birds chirping and the leaves rustling in the trees above. At that moment, I felt peaceful, like I was exactly where I was meant to be. But then, Michael's face crashed into my thoughts like a wrecking ball.

"You said you had family in New York?" I asked, trying to push away the intrusive thoughts and focusing on my first encounter with Elliott.

He took a sip of coffee before he spoke. "Actually, in Connecticut. My mom lives in New Haven. I grew up there. We moved from England when I was about ten or so," he explained.

*Of fucking course.* I was getting involved with another rich boy?

"And no, I didn't attend Yale. I wasn't smart enough." He laughed. "But my father was a professor there. My mom was a therapist before she retired. We made out okay, but we definitely didn't live in the nicest neighborhood," he went on.

*Okay, this is better.*

"Do you have siblings?" I asked curiously.

"Two sisters—twins. They're twelve years younger than me. Katherine and Kennedy." He smiled as he looked down at me; I could tell he thought fondly of them. "What about you? No, an only child, you said?"

He remembered. "Probably better that way," I joked.

Elliott was quiet as he squeezed my thigh.

"It's somehow easier to talk about Michael than my parents. I don't remember them much," I explained.

He looked down at me and his gaze sharpened.

"It's weird to say his name; I called him Daddy. He was only ten years older than me but...he liked me calling him that." I couldn't believe how easy it was for me to talk about. "He would call me his sweet girl. Sweet Jackie. His little girl. I ate it up, of course."

Elliott tensed. "Did you like calling him that?" he asked curiously.

I eyed him; I wondered what his dominant name of choice was.

"Yes," I admitted.

I waited for him to offer information.

"I was wondering if it would be too weird for you to call me that, with the age difference and all. Now I know that's probably not a good idea," he observed.

I shook my head. "I would call you anything you wanted me to," I breathed, the heat rising between my thighs.

Elliott's expression suggested his mind was racing as he glanced down at me.

He hesitated before asking, "What more did you have to tell me?"

I turned my gaze across the yard, watching the trees rustling gently in the light wind.

"After Michael did all of that to me, I still begged him to stay. I tried to kill myself once I realized he was tiring of me," I explained, my tone somehow emotionless. "I followed him on more than one occasion after he dumped me. I was...stalker level." I looked up at Elliott, ashamed. "I was very fucking naive and very fucked up in the head."

He placed his coffee on the table in front of us, then gently cupped my face and shook his head. "You were holding onto someone you thought you loved. There's nothing to be ashamed of, Jacqueline. You put him behind bars through your own strength."

I looked down, tears streaming down my face. "But I didn't. That wasn't me who put him behind bars. He kidnapped and tortured the woman he found after me. They wouldn't even listen to my story. Not that I could tell it anyway."

Elliott held me as I sobbed into his chest, the weight of shame and guilt overwhelming me once more. After a moment, he sighed heavily. "How long did he get?"

I looked up at him through tear-soaked eyes and shook my head. "Honestly, I don't know. Why?"

His eyes sharpened with a flicker of something I couldn't quite decipher. "I don't know. I'm sorry," he said gently, his expression softening.

"I want to forget about him." I dried my eyes with the back of my hand and flung my leg over him as I straddled him, grinding my hips. The desire I felt for him overpowered any thoughts I had about Michael.

Elliott grabbed my hips and helped me grind against him; I felt his cock hardening underneath my pussy, the fabric of his boxer briefs and thin joggers the only thing separating us. I pressed my lips against his and a moan escaped his throat, making me squirm as I continued to grind on him.

He pulled his lips from mine. "Get up, Jacqueline. Let me fuck you like the good girl that you are."

My heart pounded wildly, his praise piercing straight to my core. I immediately stood up, ready and waiting for his next command. He stood up and dropped his pants and boxer briefs to the ground. He gently put his hand to the side of my neck and pressed his lips to the other side.

"Tell me if you want me to stop, baby. What would you like your safe word to be?"

"Red," I breathed.

I knew my safe word would be honored with Elliott.

"And your hard limits?" His eager eyes scanned my face, as if assessing whether I was comfortable with this or not.

Did I even have hard limits anymore?

"I...I don't know. I'll let you know with my safe word." My voice was shaky. "I want this. I really want it," I assured him with a nod.

He smiled. "On your knees." His voice was deep and sultry and I immediately dropped down in front of him.

"Does my good girl want me to fuck her mouth?"

A thrill ran through me. This was a side of Elliott that I was enjoying very, very much.

"Yes, please," I breathed as I stared up at him.

"And what's my good girl going to call me?" he asked as he put his thumb to my lips, parting them.

I smiled. "Daddy."

I needed the word to be positive again, because calling Elliott Daddy made my pussy drenched.

He suddenly pushed the head of his cock into my mouth, his eyes wild with lust as he tried to thrust in and out of my mouth. I widened further, getting him down only a little bit, his size too much for my mouth. I moaned as he pulled his shirt over his head, revealing his glorious body. He threw it on the ground and pulled his cock out of my mouth, then softly slapped each cheek with it, the weight of it making my mouth water.

He smiled as I turned and licked his shaft up and down, keeping my hands on my thighs to steady myself.

"You're so eager for Daddy's cock, aren't you?"

He sounded pleased and I nodded as I looked up at him.

"Yes, Daddy. I want your cock so badly," I purred.

He licked his lower lip and then held his hands out for me to take. He lifted me up and pressed his lips against mine as he cupped my pussy with his strong hand and easily slid his middle finger inside of me. I gasped as I held my hands on his arms, trying to lift my hips up to him for more.

"You have no idea what you do to me, baby," he murmured, gently pulling my hair to force my head back and meet his eyes with mine. "I want to pound you until you scream Daddy's name for the whole neighborhood to hear."

My jaw dropped before I bit down hard on my lip. "Please, Daddy. I've been such a good girl. I need your pounding."

He grunted as he took my thighs, lifted me up, and carried me to the table behind the loveseat. He sat me down, pushed me onto my back, then lifted my shirt over my head and crafted restraints that held my wrists together. I was suddenly very aware of my completely naked body being exposed.

"Still good, baby?" he asked as he looked down at me, taking my breasts with his hands.

Oddly enough, I was. I didn't think I'd ever let anyone do this to me again, but Elliott was so astonishingly different from Michael. I had no ounce of fear in my body as I nodded and smiled up at him.

"Good. Keep your hands above your head," he ordered, then got to his knees and spread open my thighs before he put them over his shoulders.

I squirmed as his hands gently traced up my outer thighs, his lips pecking up my inner thigh towards my pussy. His hot breath lingered over my pubic bone; I looked down at him and he smiled up at me before pressing his mouth on my waxed, bare lips. My nipples hardened and my chest heaved as I stared down at him, his eyes locked onto mine.

"How quickly do you think Daddy can make you come?" He trailed his lips over vulva, so gently that I could barely feel it.

"Very quickly, Daddy," I answered, my voice barely audible.

"I had planned on teasing you, baby, but I can't fucking resist you." His mouth was suddenly buried in my pussy, his tongue swirling my clit, his fingers digging inside of me quickly.

"Oh, fuck!" I breathed out.

"Mmmm," he moaned, lapping around my pussy, practically making out with it.

The tension built quickly and I desperately lifted my hips up and down as I chased my orgasm, moaning loudly into the cool, morning air.

He parted his lips from me quickly. "Come again, baby. Keep going." He buried his face back onto me and continued to stimulate my clit while fucking me with his fingers.

"Fuck, yes!" I moaned again and felt the build of another orgasm approaching.

Suddenly I was coming again, then again, my legs trembling on his shoulders as he chuckled and parted his lips from me. He quickly pulled my legs towards him and stood me up; my restrained hands fell down in front of me as I stood and Elliott swiftly turned me around and bent me over the table.

"You are so beautiful, Jacqueline," he observed quietly as he smoothed his hands over my ass. "I keep wanting to take my time with you but I can't seem to resist your body."

"Don't take your time. Just fuck me," I breathed, wanting him to fill me up and give me the pounding he promised.

He chuckled and then his hand quickly tapped my ass, his spank startling me as I gasped and turned my head toward him.

"Such a naughty girl with that mouth of yours. Do you think you need another spanking?"

My eyes closed as I smiled, basking in his words. His deep voice continued to turn me on.

"Yes, Daddy, I do." I nodded, slightly pushing my ass out.

He let out another deep chuckle before spanking my other

ass cheek and I gasped again, opening my eyes to try to turn and look at him. My mouth salivated as I watched him stroking himself, his hand still gently caressing my ass.

"Now be a good girl and take your pounding from Daddy." He was suddenly inside of me, grabbing my hips and thrusting his hips in an increasingly rapid motion.

"Oh, fuck, yes!" I screamed, his cock pressing against my g-spot perfectly.

Elliott's hand gripped my hair and pulled back as he grunted loudly and pressed his fingertips into my hips.

"Come on, baby. Come for me again. Scream out for Daddy while I come inside of you."

He continued to fuck me quickly, his pounds deep and erratic as he bent over and began to rub my clit.

"Oh my God. Yes. Yes, Daddy. I'm coming—fuck, I'm coming," I cried out in pleasure, my pussy spasming on his cock just as he began to grunt even louder, his deep moans intensifying the heat of the moment.

His hips began to slow as I caught my breath, and I could feel his cum dripping down my leg. The only sounds I could hear were the birds chirping overhead and both of our breaths evening out.

"How was that, baby? Did everything feel good? Anything you didn't like?" He was still inside me as he gently kissed my shoulder and began to remove the shirt from my wrists.

I smiled and lifted myself up, not wanting him to leave my body. The fact that he was concerned about my wellbeing after knowing my history gave my heart a little tug.

I nodded, my back pressed against his chest as I placed my hands on his strong arms. "Everything was perfect, Elliott."

He gently kissed my shoulder once more before he took my

hands with his, interlocking them together.

"Why don't we shower and go get brunch?"

I nodded, our fingertips grazing over my body. My defenses had crumbled, and though I knew I should be terrified, I wasn't. I had never wanted anyone or anything more in my life, and I began to embrace it.

"I'd love that."

# Then

I woke up alone and groggy in the hospital, my arm bandaged and aching. A surge of horror gripped me as I realized my other arm was handcuffed to the side of the bed. The rapid beeping of my heart rate monitor intensified my panic, flooding my body with sheer fear.

"Hello? Hello? Can someone come in here, please?" I called out, tears already streaming down my face.

A nurse entered with a uniformed police officer, who stood by the door. The nurse approached my bedside, adjusting the IV bags.

"What's going on?" I asked, my voice trembling as I looked at her.

"You were brought in because you hurt yourself, Jacqueline. You're lucky your boyfriend was there to help. You cut yourself pretty deep," she explained curtly.

I looked over at the officer. "But why am I cuffed to the bed? Am I being arrested for trying to kill myself?" I asked with confusion.

He shook his head. "Michael Barnes notified the police that you were also attempting to stab him."

My mouth flew wide open in shock. "What? That's insane. I would never hurt him!"

"Honey, keep your voice down," the nurse scolded.

"But they have it all wrong! I didn't try to hurt Michael. Where is he? I need to see him!" I tugged on the handcuffs with my sore arm, trying to break free.

"Calm down, Miss Olsen!"

"I will not fucking calm down! Let me out of here! I need to see Michael!" I sobbed, my panic escalating. My breathing quickened, and I could feel a panic attack looming.

"We have a code gray on our 5150 in room 407," the nurse announced as I writhed in emotional agony.

"I need Michael!" I cried, my breaths coming in shallow gasps as I began to hyperventilate.

I felt a flurry of activity around me and a sharp prick in my cuffed arm. My eyes fluttered open just in time to see the police officer's disdained scowl before the sedative took effect. As the world faded away, I drifted into a dreamless, terrified sleep.

# Now

I couldn't believe how easy it was to be naked around Elliott. His perfect, naked body sent a shock straight to my pussy whenever I looked at him, but he somehow made me feel as if I were just as desirable. He looked down at my body in the shower all lathered in soap and then looked up at me through his lashes, desire clear in his eyes. I playfully began to stroke him and it ended up being a thirty minute shower with me having to wash myself clean again.

I stood in a towel in the middle of his room as he got dressed. "I don't have any clothes to wear."

He pulled a shirt over his head as he smiled. "Just wear mine."

I rolled my eyes. "You're 6'1" and like, a million gorgeous pounds of muscle. You think your pants are going to fit on my 5'4" pudgy body?"

He quickly raised his eyebrows. "Pudgy? That's not exactly the word I'd use to describe your body."

I put my hand to my hip. "Stocky? Soft?" I teased.

I knew I wasn't rail thin and my confidence and self-esteem plummeted ever since Michael had called my body "soft."

Elliott's eyebrows twitched as he slowly approached me. He took my hand and held it as he gazed at me softly.

"I would use...beautiful, sexy, amazing, breathtaking, exquisite. Would you like me to go on?"

I bit my lip to refrain from crying. Would I ever get used to compliments again? My initial response was to roll my eyes and scoff, but his genuineness made me stop myself. He was *so* sweet and *so* caring and *so* fucking gorgeous.

"How are you real?" I wondered aloud.

He gave me a small smile. "How are you real?" he asked softly. "You have no idea how fucking spectacular you are, Jacqueline."

I quickly smiled and then gave him a fake gasp. "Elliott! Language!"

He laughed and suddenly hoisted me over his shoulder. "You bring it out of me, you and your sailor mouth." He laughed as he playfully threw me down on the bed. "Now, before I lift your legs and stuff my cock into you again, why don't we stop by your place and get some clothes?"

I bit my lip and nodded. "Yes, Daddy."

\* \* \*

We walked into the hostel, and two of my roommates sitting in the lobby stared wide-eyed as they checked Elliott out. I grabbed his hand and led him upstairs, relieved to find my room empty.

"This is nice," Elliott said, glancing around with interest.

"It is. For now," I replied, shrugging on a long-sleeved shirt as I quickly changed out of his T-shirt and baggy joggers.

Elliott crossed his arms and watched me with a curious expression. "How long do you plan to stay here?"

I glanced at him as I pulled my jeans on. "I don't know. I

## NOW

need to start looking for a place soon now that I have a job. I'm sure I could afford my own room somewhere." I shrugged.

I grabbed a light jacket from my closet and locked it back up.

"Why don't you stay with me?" Elliott suggested.

I turned around, my eyes widening at the sincerity in his expression.

"Am I being creepy again?" he asked, a slow smile spreading across his lips.

I shook my head. "I can't do that, Elliott. This is already...a lot for me." I tried to be as gentle as possible, but he had to understand that his proposal felt absurd—he hardly knew me.

He quickly nodded. "I know. I'm sorry. That's...much too forward." He seemed disappointed but not upset.

"We'd have to get married first before moving in together," I quipped dryly.

Elliott's lips parted, but he didn't speak—did he think I was serious?

I quickly laughed. "I'm fucking with you. Come on." I headed for the door and held my hand out to him.

"Don't tempt me," he said, grabbing my hand. "I was about to run to the jewelry shop to buy you a ring," he teased back.

My heart melted. *At this point, I don't think I'd say no.*

\* \* \*

"So can you tell me what exactly is a pleasure dom? And a rigger?"

We had just ordered our brunch at a cozy cafe near Elliott's house. Sitting by the window, the morning light made his blue eyes sparkle. He leaned in, elbows on the table, as if about to share a secret.

"A pleasure dom is a dominant that derives pleasure from making their submissive feel good," he explained, his deep voice making my heart skip a beat.

I gulped and nodded. "I like that."

"And a rigger enjoys tying up their subs. I'm not sure how you'd feel about that, and I'm completely okay with not doing it if you're not comfortable," he said sincerely.

I took a moment to think. I felt safe with Elliott. When he used his shirt to restrain me earlier that day, I felt nothing but desire. With Michael, there was fear always laced with desire. But I wanted to explore with Elliott, especially since he was so invested and concerned about my wellbeing.

"I would be willing to explore that with you." I nodded. "You make me feel safe, Elliott. You make me feel good about myself. And it's easy to do anything with you and that fucking body of yours." Of course, I had to add something in to make the moment less serious.

He smiled and reached his hands out to me. I looked down at our hands as I extended mine, our fingers intertwining perfectly, his large hands enveloping mine with ease.

"I care about you a lot, Jacqueline. I want to move at a pace you're comfortable with."

My eyes started to well with tears. "You have no idea how much that means to me."

If it were up to me, with a guaranteed happily ever after, I'd move into his house, get married, and never leave his side. Right then and there. But nothing was guaranteed. And as much as I wanted my happily ever after, I was afraid I would somehow fuck it all up and he would end up hurting me, leaving scars that I'd never recover from.

# Then

I lay in my hospital bed, curled up in a fetal position. On day two of my seventy-two-hour involuntary psychiatric hold, the medication left me feeling groggy and numb. I couldn't keep any food down, and the relentless drowsiness made every minute feel like an eternity.

I was notified that Michael was not going to press charges against me. *Duh, I didn't do anything wrong.* Did he just want to scare me? I had no idea if I would ever see him again, not after what he said I tried to do to him. Did I somehow forget that I tried to stab the love of my life? Why would I do that? All I wanted was to get his attention. And apparently that hadn't even worked. I thought he would at least come and visit me and confess his undying love to me. But after my seventy-two-hour hold, the psychologist on site declared I was safe to go home under the supervision of a therapist. And Michael never walked through the visitor doors.

I endlessly called and texted him in the following days. I knew I had fucked everything up. *How am I supposed to live now? The only person that gave a shit about me is fucking ghosting me.* He was leaving me just like everyone else had. But I couldn't give up. I had to fight to win him back. He needed to see that no one would ever love him the way I did.

I watched Michael walk into his office building, just as I had been doing for the past week. My heart dropped every single time I saw him ignoring my call. I started to panic. I couldn't take it anymore—I needed to speak to him. I rushed into his building on the chilly November morning, my heart pounding as I searched for him. As I waited for the elevator to reach the lobby, I caught a glimpse of him approaching from the corner of my eye.

"Jackie, come. Follow me," he instructed, holding his hand out for me.

I was both surprised and overjoyed as I took his hand. He pulled me into the stairwell and quietly shut the door behind us. He glanced up the stairwell before shoving me against the door, his hand pressing firmly against my throat.

"You need to leave me the fuck alone. Stop fucking following me. Stop fucking calling and texting me. You need to move the fuck on, Jackie," he spit out, his gray eyes dark and angry with a vein popping out of his temple.

I began to sob as he quickly let go of me and straightened his jacket up.

"Why don't you love me anymore?" I cried, trying to be quiet so I wouldn't upset him further.

Michael just laughed—he fucking laughed out loud in my face.

"You really thought I could love someone as vile as you? Jesus Christ, Jackie. You're pathetic," he hissed.

Now I was angry. "Then why did you fucking tell me that you did? Why did you scar my skin with your name? Why did you give me a fucking ring?" I didn't care about my tone anymore; I was yelling now, my voice echoing in the empty stairwell.

He smiled sinisterly. "Because you were so easy to manipulate. You were so eager, and for what? You cured my boredom. You were an easy fuck." He shrugged nonchalantly, as if dismissing my very existence. "I knew you wouldn't turn on me, even when I did all of that to you. You were just *so* fucking pathetic, Jackie."

I shook my head, words unable to form in my mouth.

"And now look at you, sweet Jackie. You're ruined. You will forever be all mine and only mine. And I will never, ever be yours."

# Now

The weekend at the restaurant was exhausting, but the generous tips were a nice reward. Still, the lack of sleep caught up with me, thanks to the late nights I spent with Elliott; he would convince me to stay with him, pick me up, and then we'd end up making out and fucking until the wee hours of the morning.

I hesitantly let Elliott know that I would be sleeping in my own bed that night. Plus, I needed to start looking for my own place, figure out how the hell I'd get my driver's license and own car, find a new therapist and in the midst of all that, forget about Michael's threatening call that I received in New York. I was certain that changing my number would solve everything.

While I scrolled through pages and pages of apartments and rooms for rent, I received a call from an unknown number. I looked at the time at the top of my screen: 11:52 p.m. *Who would be calling me at this time? Elliott?* Too curious, I answered.

"Hello?" I crept out of the room so I wouldn't wake any roommates.

"Sweet Jackie."

My heart began to bang in my chest as fear spread throughout my body.

"What do you want? How did you get this number?" I was surprised at how calm and assertive I was being.

"I have my ways. Don't you miss me?" There was a smile clear in his voice.

I started shaking and my knees began to buckle.

"Why are you calling me?" I asked, my voice becoming weaker.

He began to chuckle. "I want to see my sweet Jackie. Daddy misses you."

I snorted. "That will never fucking happen."

"No? How do you know I've not already seen you? How's Los Angeles, by the way?"

I began to tremble and immediately hung up.

"What the fuck?" I cried to myself, tears streaming down my face.

He started calling back, but I turned my phone off immediately. My mind raced with panic: *how did he get my new number? Is he in LA? Is he watching me? Why does he still want to torment me after all these years?*

"Fuck this." I went back into my room, grabbed my coat and purse, then headed down the street to Zee's bar.

I walked in wearing leggings and Elliott's flannel jacket, which made me look like a kid in a trench coat. It was past midnight on Sunday, but the place was still packed. I spotted Zee behind the bar, and she excitedly waved when she saw me coming.

"Hey! You're back!" Her smile was infectious.

"Yeah, I—I've had a rough night. Can I get a vodka seven?" I asked, almost apologetically.

"Of course." Her smile softened with understanding as she started making my drink.

She was quick to place my drink in front of me.

"Thanks. I'm Jackie, by the way," I said, feeling bad about

not greeting her in a friendlier manner.

"Nice to formally meet you, Jackie. So, why the bad night?" She put her elbows on the bar and intently waited for my answer.

I sighed and shook my head before I took a few gulps of my drink. "I was contacted by someone from my past. Someone... someone that abused me."

Her mouth dropped in shock. "Fuck. Are you okay?" Her concern was evident, and she looked genuinely upset on my behalf.

I shook my head, taking a long sip of my drink. "Nope. Can I get another one?"

I quickly drank two more and became acquainted with Zee; I welcomed her friendly distraction. She was born and raised in LA, she just turned thirty-two, she had been a bartender for ten years and was sober for nine. I thought it was strange that she still wanted to be around alcohol every day when she was sober. I told her about moving back to LA because of the ominous phone call, about meeting Elliott, and we bonded over our love for David Bowie.

The bar was starting to clear the closer that 2 a.m. approached. I was four drinks in and not wanting to go back to my room alone. I wanted Elliott but I didn't want him to see me drunk. I was already on the verge of tears and I didn't want to talk about Michael, even though I knew that would inevitably be brought up because drunk Jackie was an even bigger mess than sober Jackie.

"Hey, let me walk you home. I can close up after," Zee offered, breaking me out of a drunken daze.

I nodded slowly and unevenly. "Okay."

I was relieved that I would have someone by my side when I

would inevitably get murdered by Michael; my drunken mind was certain he was watching me at that very moment.

I stumbled off my seat and put my coat on, following Zee out the back door. She had her arm wrapped around my shoulders as we walked toward the main street, the cold air hitting me with a wave of surprise.

"I thought California was supposed to be warm," I slurred out, suddenly laughing.

Zee kindly laughed beside me as she pulled her phone out.

"I mean, it's forty-six degrees. Aren't you used to that kind of weather?" she teased.

I shrugged. "I guess. I'm just like…I'm so fucking angry," I murmured, my mind already on Michael. "Who does he think he is? He's just a fucking rich boy that hates women. You look like her. She was very kind to me." My thoughts were all over the place and I knew it even in my drunken state.

"Like who?" Zee asked, looking both ways as we crossed the street.

"Hana. The girl he kidnapped," I stated dryly.

I could feel her eyes on me now. "Jesus Christ. And this fucker is out of jail now?"

I didn't even realize I had told her about that.

"Yes. He's probably here now." I shrugged. "I don't know why."

We finally reached the front of my building, and Zee let out a loud sigh. "Are you sure you don't wanna crash at my place?" she offered.

I laughed for some reason. "No, I mean, I'll be fine."

That's when I saw Elliott walk out of my building with a look of surprise and concern.

"Where have you been? I've been calling you, Jacqueline,"

he said as he quickly wrapped his arms around me.

"I assume you're Elliott?" Zee asked him.

"Yes. You are?" he asked curiously.

"I'm Zee. I'm glad you're here. She's spooked about that fucker Michael," she explained.

I groaned in Elliott's chest; now I was definitely going to have to explain what happened.

He looked down at me. "What happened, baby?"

"See ya guys," I heard Zee say as she walked off.

Elliott looked back at her as he walked us into the lobby. "Thank you for getting her here safely."

I immediately broke down in tears. "Michael called me. He said he wanted to see me and that he knew I was in LA. I have no fucking idea how he got my number," I sobbed.

Elliott looked around and at the front desk receptionist.

"Let's get your things. You're staying with me." He took my hand and guided me up the stairs.

"*All* of my things?" I asked as I carefully followed him, holding the wall.

"Yes. You'll be safe with me, Jacqueline."

*God, I love the way he says my name.* I almost forgot about everything else going on as I listened to his deep, calming voice.

"I already paid until the end of the week though," I argued.

I knew that if I began to stay with him, I would never want to leave.

He looked back at me with a small smile. "I'll pay you back for it."

I groaned again and we stopped in the hallway leading to the room.

"Elliott, I can't. I don't even...I can't," I stammered, struggling to find the right words. My fear was overwhelming, not

## NOW

just about staying with him but also about Michael.

"Jacqueline," he whispered, looking down at me and taking my hands. "He called me too. That's why I came looking for you."

My heart began to race wildly again. "What?" My voice trembled. "What did he say?"

Elliott sighed deeply. "It doesn't matter. He was just trying to mess with me."

I began to cry, but then I thought of a deal. "*Please* tell me, Elliott. And then I'll come stay with you."

He scanned my face, concern clear in his eyes. "He asked me why I still wanted you when you were his."

I scoffed. "What did you say?"

I was sobering up real quick.

Elliott hesitated before he answered. "I told him to fuck off and if he came anywhere near you, I'd kill him. Then I hung up."

My mouth dropped. I knew at that moment that I was in love with him.

"Thank you. Let me go get my things."

# Then

I continued to follow Michael, unsure of what I hoped to achieve. Maybe I wanted revenge, but I didn't know how. What could I even do? I had nothing on him. Who would believe me if I tried to tell someone what he did? A part of me still loved him—a big part. He was all I had left, even if he hated me. I couldn't imagine living without him because, in a twisted way, he was right—I would always be his.

He began leaving work with a beautiful blonde who always wore bold red lipstick. They would wait until they were a couple of blocks away before intertwining their fingers, a gesture he never showed me in public. They even went to his apartment together. My heart would leap into my throat as I spent hours waiting outside his building, only to realize she wasn't leaving. What was so different about her? Was she the reason he grew tired of me? I planned on confronting her one day after work. I didn't know when, but I would figure it out when the time came.

I had just sat down on a bench in Battery Park near his work when I saw her. She seemed to be waiting for someone as she looked around and then sat at a bench nearby. I couldn't believe the opportunity had just laid itself out in front of me.

"Jackie." His voice was already menacing.

## THEN

I looked back and Michael was standing almost directly behind me.

"Sit back, Jackie. You don't deserve to look at me."

I obeyed and slowly sat back.

"Who is she?" I spit out, already angry and hurt and jealous.

He ignored me. "I told you to stop stalking me. Don't think I don't see you following me."

I started to look back again, but he slammed his hand onto my shoulder, shoving me back into place with a forceful grip.

"Do not approach her. Do not talk to her. If you so much as look at her again, I will fucking kill you."

I gasped, struggling to catch my breath between quiet sobs.

"Leave *now*, Jackie."

I immediately stood up as an attractive man approached Michael's blonde and wrapped her in a hug. I paused, transfixed by the sight.

"*Now!*"

Tears continued to stream down my face as I walked away, unable to even glance at Michael. From the corner of my eye, I saw him lean against a tree, his gaze fixed intently on her.

I walked across the street and into Starbucks for a job interview. My plan was strategic; if I worked there, Michael couldn't scold me for being in the area. With him no longer taking care of me, I had to start fending for myself again. I couldn't give up on him just yet. Because if I couldn't have him, then nobody could.

# Now

I woke up in Elliott's bed with a massive hangover. It took me a moment to piece together the events of the previous night. Fuck—Michael.

"Well, good morning, beautiful," Elliott said, walking in with a coffee in hand. He leaned against the door frame, a warm smile spreading across his face.

"Good morning," I croaked, my voice raspy and worn as if I'd smoked a thousand cigarettes the night before.

He sat on the bed beside me and started brushing back the hair in my face. "How are you feeling?"

I smiled and let out a laugh. "Like hell," I admitted.

He gave me a slight frown as he paused. "Why didn't you call me the second you heard from Michael?"

I shut my eyes tight and sighed. "Because I didn't want to burden you with this."

As I opened my eyes, Elliott was shaking his head.

"Jacqueline...you will never be a burden," he said softly. "Don't you realize how much I care about you?"

I blinked away tears and shook my head. "I care about you so much. That's why I'm scared. I'm scared that I'm going to lose you and I'm scared of what Michael will do to us," I admitted as I sat up, my head throbbing.

## NOW

He gazed at me for a while, seemingly in deep thought. "You will never have to be scared with me. Trust me, Jacqueline." His voice was low and deep and sent a wave of desire throughout my body.

I nodded. I believed him.

"I'm going to figure out how Michael got your contact information. We'll go from there."

I looked down at the ground, confused. I looked back up at him with a wary smile. "How are you going to figure that out?"

Elliott hesitated. "I'm...I have some contacts that can help with that," he assured me.

I raised my eyebrows. "Oh yeah? Some fellow therapist contacts?"

He laughed and nodded. "Something like that."

\* \* \*

Elliott went into his office to take some video sessions with his clients. He told me he didn't want to leave me so he was going to work from home. Luckily, I had the day off so I slept for a few more hours while he worked. I didn't bother to turn my phone back on; the only person I wanted to talk to was in the next room anyway.

When I woke up, I felt significantly better. Elliott's voice drifted in from the other room, reminding me that I was safe. My luggage, now tucked in the corner, served as a stark reminder that I was moving in with him. It was surreal—just two weeks ago, I had met the Nice Hot Older Guy on the plane, and now here I was, about to fucking live with him.

He wasn't just any guy; he was *the* guy, or at least, I was convinced he was. But the reality of moving in with him scared me. Things couldn't always be this perfect, and I feared the moment he'd discover my darker, clingy side. I'd been meticulously hiding that part of me, but living together meant it was only a matter of time before it surfaced.

Elliott seemed so put-together—his own house, a stable career. I couldn't help but question what I had to offer. What if he saw me as nothing more than a hopeless mess? What would I bring to the table?

"Hey." Elliott walked in, snapping me out of my spiraling thoughts. "You okay?"

I blinked, trying to think of an answer. "I'm sort of freaking out about staying here. I mean...I *am* freaking out. What if you end up thinking I'm a lunatic and then you're just stuck with me?"

He paused and then smiled. "I'm well trained to handle lunatics," he teased.

I smiled but quickly shook my head and raised my shoulders, tense as I stood up. "Seriously. I am definitely like, sort of a lunatic. I'm gonna be needy and need constant validation and I will probably annoy you with how much I stare at you because you're so fucking gorgeous."

He started to walk towards me, his gaze tender and reassuring. "I love all of those things about you, Jacqueline." He placed his hand gently on my cheek, his smile soft and sincere.

My heart sank to my belly. "Even the staring?" I joked quietly, too mesmerized by his eyes and the fact that he said he *loved* things about me.

"We can have a nightly staring contest," he teased back.

"I'd win, for sure," I quipped.

He smiled and pulled me in for a kiss—a tender, sweet, and loving kiss that made my heart skip a beat. As his lips met

## NOW

mine, a warm wave of bliss enveloped my entire body, melting away all my doubts and fears. His kiss was soft yet full of an indescribable depth. When he finally pulled away, I had to catch my breath, my cheeks flushed and my pulse racing. It was possibly the best kiss I had ever experienced, and I found myself craving more.

"At least let me pay rent." Of course, I had to ruin the moment.

He seemed to think for a moment, his gaze softening as he looked at me. "I'm not going to take your money," he said sweetly, his tone reassuring. But I couldn't let it go that easily.

"Please. I don't want you to think I'm taking advantage of you, or for me to just... feel guilty about this," I insisted, shaking my head. "I want to contribute in some way. It's important to me."

He licked his lips and glanced out the window, his expression thoughtful. Then he took my hand and guided me to the bed, sitting down and drawing me onto his lap. As he settled me against him, he gently rubbed his hand over my thigh, his touch soothing despite the visible scars. He didn't even seem to notice them.

"You won't budge on this, will you?" he asked with a teasing smile, his fingers tracing comforting patterns on my skin.

I shook my head with a smile of my own, feeling a warmth spread through me. "Nope."

He sighed. "Okay. Will you still...sleep in this bed with me?" he asked, almost shyly.

"I would love that." I grinned, then glanced at the bed. "You sure you're okay with me taking this side?"

I wasn't sure how to phrase it—whether he was ready for me to share the space that had once been Kate's. I didn't want to intrude on the memories.

He nodded as our eyes met.

"I'm ready," he said softly, as if he understood my unspoken concerns.

I gave him another one of our sweet, tender kisses that gradually heated up; I wrapped my leg around him, straddling him as our kiss deepened. But just as things were getting intense, he pulled his lips away.

His eyes were filled with a mix of vulnerability and determination. "Before we go any further, I need to tell you something," he said, his voice trembling slightly. "And I don't want to scare you off, but... I need you to know this."

My stomach tightened, the warmth between us suddenly overshadowed by the weight of his words.

"I love you, Jacqueline. You don't need to say it back. I just needed you to know, because I'm not going anywhere."

There was an immediate lump in my throat. *Thank God he said it first.* I was overwhelmed with relief and love, and I must have looked like a lunatic, grinning through my tears.

"I love you too, Elliott."

# Then

I was starting to get more bold. I would purposely hang around Battery Park, waiting for a glimpse of Michael and his mystery blonde. I would go all the way up to the East Village from Park Slope just to watch Michael walk to the bodega down the street. And he knew I was still following and watching him; he would constantly make eye contact with me and stare at me as he held blondie's hand. He knew it would hurt me so he continued his affection with her. I wondered if she was also his submissive. Didn't he *not* have romantic relationships with anyone? Or was that just with his submissives? Did those two ever intertwine?

I wasn't sleeping when Michael called me at 2 a.m. one morning. I sat on my bed in the dark, trying to hack into his email to see if I could get any information about blondie that way.

"M—Michael?" I answered, confused.

His tone was instantly harsh. "Why are you trying to get into my email?"

I began to sob immediately. "Because I love you. And I miss you," I cried.

He sighed heavily. "My sweet Jackie. Don't cry."

I stopped crying and my heart dropped to the floor. "I'm still your sweet Jackie?"

He laughed to himself. "Of course you are. Isn't my name scarred into your skin?" He made it sound like that was something romantic.

I looked down at his name on my leg. "But..." I wasn't sure how to go on.

"Is your pussy wet for Daddy?" His voice was low and he almost sounded drunk. That didn't stop my heart from beating wildly in my chest as my pussy throbbed with need. *Daddy.*

"Always, Daddy," I breathed into the phone.

There was a sound on his end that seemed like he had just closed a car door.

"Go to your front door. Close the door behind you and get on your knees."

My lips parted, unsure of what was going on. *Is he here?*

"Do you understand?" He sounded angry.

"Y—yes, Daddy."

He hung up.

I jumped up, bolted out of my room and headed straight to the front door. *Am I getting him back? Will I be his again?* I closed the door behind my back and got to my knees. I thought my heart might fly out of my chest as I waited. And then I saw his familiar figure walk up the stairs.

"Eyes on the ground." His voice was as cold and harsh as ever.

My eyes went to the floor in front of me. It was clear by the smell of alcohol on him that he was not sober.

"Stand up and face the wall. Do not look at me."

My legs quivered as I stood, my gaze fixed on the wall. My hands shook uncontrollably as I pressed them to the sides of my trembling thighs.

Michael abruptly pulled my pajama shorts and underwear

down and then locked my hands behind my back with his grip. I could hear him pull his zipper down before he quickly thrust himself into me. A surprised gasp escaped my mouth as he pounded me against the wall. He took his free hand and covered my mouth, then whispered in my ear.

"Be quiet, sweet Jackie. Let Daddy come in you like a good girl."

My body melted with his praise as he continued, his pumps quickening.

It only took a minute for him to groan into my neck and I realized he was coming. I wasn't even upset that he didn't let me come—I was just happy that he fucked me.

He didn't stay inside me for long. He pulled out and quickly zipped his pants back up, but he still held my wrists behind my back. He lifted my shorts up and then put his mouth softly against my ear.

"Don't you dare think this means anything." His tone was angry again, a familiar edge creeping into his voice. "I just needed to come and you were the easiest fuck. Now go back to bed and keep my cum inside of you."

He released his grip and I turned to face him. The side of my head and my body suddenly pounded against the wall with his force as he pressed his body against mine.

"You are not to look at me. Go inside. Now."

He released me and I began to quietly cry. I put my hand on the doorknob and paused; he was still there.

"I love you, Daddy," I whispered to the door.

"Shut the fuck up and go inside, Jackie."

My heart dropped and felt like it was torn apart as I opened the door and shut it behind me. I put my ear to the door and heard his footsteps gradually disappear as he went down the stairs. I slowly walked back to my room, his cum dripping down my leg, and went to sleep.

# Now

Days had passed since receiving the call from Michael. I continued to wonder how Elliott would figure out who had called and what was going on, but I trusted him. It was a strange feeling to trust someone so completely again. But it wasn't blind trust, was it? Elliott made me feel like the most important person in the world and he was trying to protect me by having me move in with him. He told me he loved me and to never be afraid with him. And I wholeheartedly accepted that. I never felt that with Michael. And I hated that I only had mine and Michael's twisted, fucked up relationship to compare it to.

Elliott picked me up from work a few nights after our "I love you" exchange. Everything was going perfectly; we spent our nights after work fucking and cuddling and then during the day, I would longingly wait for him to be done with his sessions so I could follow him around like a fly. Only he happily took this fly to lunch and fingered me in his car while waiting in the LA traffic.

As we pulled up to the house and Elliott cut the engine, I blurted out, "I want you to tie me up."

He looked over at me with a mischievous grin. "Are you sure?"

I nodded with my head held high. I was nervous, but it was a *good* nervous; I was eager to see more of Elliott's dominant side.

There was a pause before he nodded and put his hand on my thigh. "Okay. Let's go inside and first discuss our boundaries."

My heart couldn't take how much I loved how respectful and mindful he was. He knew exactly what he was doing.

I changed into one of Elliott's shirts and we sat at the dining table as if we were conducting a business meeting. I nervously bit my lip as I clasped my hands underneath the table.

"Don't be nervous, baby. I want to make sure you get the most pleasure out of this." He smiled at me, finding my hands with his.

"I know. I'm excited, honestly. So, um...yeah, let's discuss!" I laughed shyly, eager to start.

He didn't hesitate to begin. "First of all, I want you to know that I have extensive knowledge with rope and binding," he explained carefully.

"Were you like a boy scout or something?" I teased; of course I could never keep a moment too serious.

Elliott laughed, his smile reaching his eyes. "I was, actually. But I have done extensive research on rigging and have years of experience with...with Kate." He seemed hesitant to talk about her in this setting.

I put my hand to his arm. "It's okay to talk about her with me. You can tell me anything."

He smiled appreciatively. "Thank you." He paused for a moment, then added, "I also want you to know that our play dynamics don't have to spill over into our relationship. Once we're done playing, you don't have to call me Daddy or be submissive."

I thought for a moment. "What if I want to?"

He instantly grinned. "Then you can." His voice made my stomach do all sorts of flips.

"Let's first discuss our safe words," he continued. "Do you have any in mind?"

I gulped and sighed, filling my lungs before I spoke. "Let's use red."

Elliott studied me carefully. "Are you sure?"

I nodded. "That was my safe word with Michael, but he never honored it. I'd like to take back that word and have it actually mean something," I explained.

I saw a flicker of anger flash through his eyes. "Okay, baby. Red it is. I will always honor your safe words," he said gently.

I noticed his use of plurals. "Is there more than one safe word I should be using?"

He shifted a little, his excitement evident as he explained, "I like to use safe words similar to a stoplight system. Red means stop everything immediately. Yellow means we need to wrap up soon or slow down. Green is 'everything is great, keep going.' Does that make sense?"

This was the first time I had heard of multiple safe words, but I liked it. "Perfectly."

"And you're good with those?" he asked, his eyes scanning my face intently, trying to read me.

More flips and spins swirled in my chest and stomach. "Yes."

His smile melted my heart. "How do you feel about impact play? Spanking, slapping, the use of objects such as floggers, paddles, riding crops?"

I was already getting turned on just talking about all of it. "I, um...I think I would enjoy it with you. I am open to it." I nodded.

"Okay." He flashed his gorgeous smile again. "We'll start out slow. Is there anywhere you aren't comfortable with me touching during our play?"

Surprisingly, I had no problem with Elliott touching my scars. He softly grazed my body with his fingers every night; he stroked my scars as if he could erase all the hurt they caused me. So frankly, he could touch me anywhere he wanted. "No. You have unlimited access to my body."

He licked his lower lip as he stared at mine. "Any hard limits? Something you absolutely don't want to do?"

I couldn't believe how detailed we were getting in this conversation. Michael just went right in and fucked me up. *So fucking naive, Jackie.*

I cleared my throat before I spoke. "I ask that you use lube for any anal play," I answered quietly.

Elliott's eyes widened. "Of course. That's a necessity." He shook his head. "Did Michael not use lube?"

I nervously bit the inside of my cheek. "At least not the first time. That's when he didn't honor my safe word." Tears were forming in my eyes and I quickly caught them at the edge of my eye before they could fall.

I saw the anger flicker across his face again. "Jesus fucking Christ," he spit out, then looked out the window beside us. "The things I'm going to do to him..."

"Please." I put my hand to his arm. "Let's not talk about him right now. Let's continue."

He looked back at me and his eyes softened.

"Okay, you're right." His voice returned to his normal gentleness. "How do you feel about suspension?"

I'm sure he could tell that I had no idea what the fuck he was talking about.

"Being bound and hung up from an overhead suspension. It's perfect for teasing and fucking you without you being able to move an inch," he explained, his deep and low voice making my pussy twitch.

I quickly nodded. "Yes. I want to try that."

He licked his lips again, his eyes darkening with desire. "Okay, good," he breathed, the words laced with a palpable longing.

I glanced down at his hard cock underneath his gray sweats. If only he could see how wet I was.

"What about a ball gag?"

I looked out the window, my heart dropping a little. "How would I use my safe word with that?"

He took my hand and gently ran his thumb across my knuckles. "A safety hum. A safety blink. A shake of the head. Whatever you are comfortable with."

That made sense. "Then yes," I answered. "I'll shake my head." It felt powerful getting to decide what *I* wanted.

"And you want to call me Daddy?" His eyes, filled with a mix of concern and desire, scanned my face intently.

I smiled. "Yes, Daddy."

He let go of my hand and slowly inched his way closer between my thighs. "Is it okay to call you baby girl? Or is that too much?" He narrowed his eyes, unsure and hesitant.

I shook my head. "No, Daddy. I want to be your good baby girl."

His chest rose up and down quickly. "Good. We've gone over enough. Let's play."

He quickly stood up and took my hand, then led me into the bedroom.

"Let's get you undressed, baby girl." He pulled my shirt

over my head and flung it to the ground. His fingers gently hooked my underwear as he pulled them down slowly. My heart thumped in my chest as he carefully grazed my breasts in his hands, looking down at me like I was the most perfect being in the world.

"I love you so much," he whispered.

"I love you too, Daddy," I said with a shaky, excited breath as I smiled.

A groan escaped his throat as he gazed at me with lustful eyes. He removed his hands from me and lifted his shirt over his head. I didn't think I'd ever tire of seeing his body unclothed. He pulled down his gray sweats, revealing his hard cock, and stepped out of them as he took my hand and led me to the bed.

"Sit," he ordered, his voice stern.

*Holy shit. Dominant Elliott.* I was fucking drenched. I immediately sat on the bed and looked up at him, waiting for my next command.

"Sit on your knees on the bed," he clarified. "Wait here while I grab my rope."

He walked into his closet as I got up and sat on the bed, desperately wanting to touch myself. Only seconds later, he walked out with rope and smiled deviously at me.

"I will be putting this around your legs and ankles into a frogtie," he explained. "And then I will be wrapping you into a boxtie."

I nodded. I had no idea what the fuck a boxtie or frogtie was but I honestly didn't care; he could put me into a fucking pretzel tie if he wanted.

I quietly observed while he put the rope carefully around my thighs and ankles. He continued to wrap it around me and I sat watching him, impressed with how easy he made it look. He went to my other leg and did the same.

"Good. Now I'll start the boxtie. I'll need your hands behind your back, holding onto each of your forearms, like this." He turned around and showed me what to do.

I smiled gratefully. "Thank you for explaining all of this to me," I said, feeling a little embarrassed.

He turned back to me with a smile. "Of course."

He turned me around so my back faced him and he began to tie the rope again. My arms were bound behind my back as he wrapped the rope around my chest above my breasts, then under them.

"It takes a lot of preparation. It's worth it though, baby girl," he explained.

I bit my lip as I let out a little giggle. There I was, giggling like a little girl again. "I know it will be." My cheeks felt red hot.

I was suddenly feeling shy and I wasn't sure why. Was it because I was in such a vulnerable position?

"Fuck, you look so good tied up for me," he mused as he finished.

My breathing hitched as his arm wrapped around my stomach and pulled me close to his chest. He began to graze his hands over my breasts, playing with my erect nipples, and I felt his erection grow on my bare ass cheek. I gasped when he pushed me down onto the bed and the side of my face landed on the soft bed. My ass was lifted in the air as my legs and thighs were bound together; I gasped with a jolt when his mouth pressed against my pussy, wasting no time swirling his tongue around my clit.

"Fuck," I moaned; I was already close to coming.

"Mmmm." His mouth vibrated into my pussy and the feeling

had my orgasm flying over the edge as I lifted my hips up and down, chasing even more pleasure.

Elliott chuckled to himself. "I love hearing you come, baby. Let's do it again." His mouth was back to my pussy and he continued to play with my clit with his tongue, sending me over the edge again, then again, until my legs began to tremble. He finally removed his mouth from my pulsing pussy and lifted me up to his chest.

"Now I want to see your face when you come." He quickly lifted me by my hips and turned me over, laying me on my back on the bed. He spread open my thighs and began to stroke himself as he stared down at me.

"You're so fucking beautiful, Jacqueline," he breathed. "I could come just by looking at you."

My heart exploded. He was so fucking sexy and no one had made me feel so desirable before.

"Please, Daddy. I want you to come," I whimpered.

He flashed a grin at me. "Not yet, baby girl. I need you to come more for me."

He suddenly pulled my thighs closer to his body and quickly thrust himself into me, the pleasure from him filling me up and pounding into me forcing out small, abrupt screams. Soon his thumb was on my clit, rubbing furiously to make me come.

"Show me, baby. Show me how much I can make you come on my cock."

His words and his touch took me to the brink of bliss, a feral scream from my throat shocking me as I came on his cock. My eyes shut tight as his thrusts didn't waver; he continued to pound me, rubbing my clit even faster, forcing another orgasm. As I came down from my high, I looked up at him and he looked so fucking hot with his body glistening with sweat, his blue eyes clouded with lust and desire.

"Good girl," he breathed before he smiled.

"Please come for me, Daddy," I begged.

I was desperate for the feeling of his cum inside of me.

I was startled as he grabbed my hips and let out a loud grunt, his deep voice growling out with pleasure. I smiled as he slowed his hips and caught his breath. His warm liquid began to slide out of me as he leaned down and gently kissed my neck, riling me up again.

"Are you ready for more, baby girl?" he whispered between soft pecks on my neck.

"Oh, fuck yes," I whimpered.

There was a sudden slap to my tit, making me gasp, as Elliott gazed down at me.

"Try that again, baby. And watch your fucking mouth." He smiled as he began to rub my clit again, his hard cock still inside of me.

"Yes, please, Daddy. Give me more," I corrected myself, my heart racing with desire.

He thrust deep inside of me and kept his cock there for a moment.

"Fuck, you feel good, baby. So fucking good." He grazed his hand up my neck and to my cheek. "I need to fuck your beautiful ass now."

Tears pricked my eyes; he felt so good—he made *me* feel so good.

He suddenly pulled out and grabbed lube from his nightstand, keeping me exposed and vulnerable, but I was eager for more. His muscled body and hard cock made my pussy pulse and yearn for more as I watched him lather himself with lube. He pulled the rope that kept my legs and ankles tied together and turned me over, face down on the bed. The cold lube trickled down my ass before he threw the bottle to the floor. Elliott grabbed the rope binding me from behind and pulled me closer to the edge of the bed.

"Remember, baby. I will honor any of your safe words. You are in control here," he whispered in my ear.

My heart stung deep in my chest. *How on Earth did I find someone who was so understanding and caring, who cared about my wellbeing and safety? Especially someone so fucking hot?*

The tip of his cock began to push into my ass. I was no stranger to anal but this felt exciting and new, especially since I hadn't done anything like it in years...not since him. *God damnit, why do I have to keep thinking of him?* Elliott slowly inched himself into me, each push making me gasp and hold my breath. He was so much bigger than Michael. *There I fucking go again thinking about him.* Finally, he was all the way inside me, and goosebumps engulfed my entire body.

"Oh my God, Daddy. You feel so good in my ass," I moaned, clenching my eyes shut.

He chuckled as he took hold of the knot between my shoulders.

"Your ass feels so good. Your body is so fucking perfect, baby," he breathed, slowly pumping his hips.

I let out little yelps as he continued to quicken the speed of his thrusts. I heard something turn on and vibrate, and I opened my eyes to see Elliott holding a small black vibrator with a clit stimulator. He easily slid the vibrator into me, and the way it hit my clit immediately had my pussy spasming and clenching around it.

"Oh my God!" I whined, my orgasms back to back as he continued to thrust deep and hard into my ass.

"You take Daddy's cock so well. Such a good girl, baby." His breaths were quick and I knew he was close to coming.

I lost count of how many times I came before Elliott grunted loudly, his primal moans making my pussy clench around the vibrator one last time. He carefully removed the vibrator and then pulled out of me.

"Still green, baby?" he asked, pecking my shoulder lightly with his lips and grazing my ass with one hand.

I smiled and nodded, dazed and elated. I was green and fucking high off his cock.

"Do you need rest? Or are you ready for more?"

*More?! Holy shit. Are we marathoning?* "Daddy, I'm always ready for more from you."

He chuckled. "Good. Because now I'm going to focus all on you."

# Then

I became even more obsessed after the night Michael came to fuck me.

I had successfully hacked into his email. I saw a confirmation email about a purchase for a ring—a submissive ring. I began to bawl; why didn't he want me anymore? Why did *she* get him now? What was so special about her? What did she have that I didn't have? I sent angry texts to Michael, desperate for him to speak to me.

**You should change your password. Who's this new submissive you're shopping for?**

He responded back quickly: **I've changed it many times, Jackie. Leave me alone.**

I shook my head to myself. **Do you love her? Did you give her the sub ring yet?**

I wanted him to know that I knew what he was up to.

**Yes, I love her. And yes, I did...but this time, I mean it.**

I began to sob. **Ouch. I give it a month. You're so quick to move on.**

I was surprised at how quickly he was responding. **Jackie, leave me the fuck alone.**

I ignored him. **Did you tell her about me yet?**

**No. You are irrelevant and unimportant.**

I was irrelevant and unimportant? Did he somehow not remember what he did to me? **That's not what you were saying a few months ago. Remember? You tied me up and told me to call you daddy.**

**That was before I knew how fucking sick you are, Jackie. Go check yourself back into Lennox Hill.**

I gasped. He was really going to call *me* sick? After he did all that shit to me?

I texted back quickly: **You're the one that put me there for fucking mutilating me. And why come back to me and fuck me if I'm so irrelevant and unimportant?**

I waited for a response as I waited for it to be delivered. My text went through, but I realized it wasn't through iMessage anymore. *Did he fucking block me?*

I wondered if he had carved his name onto her too. I needed to find out more about this mystery blonde. I knew exactly what to do.

I was now an expert at stalking people. It wasn't hard to figure out who she was. I went to the New York Daily website and looked at all the articles. I clicked on every woman's name, googled it, and continued my search when it wasn't her. Then I found Hana Miller. She had written something about a woman with an eating disorder. I googled her name, and there popped up the mystery blonde. She was even more beautiful up close. Her Instagram was filled with pictures of books, sunsets, and views of the city. She apparently lived in Williamsburg. I found a selfie of her standing against greenery, a crooked smile on her red lips.

I needed to seek her out and tell her about Michael. I had a plan and everything: I would follow her home, knock on her door, and spill everything. I'd show her my scars. I'd tell her that he came to me one night, fucking me even though they were apparently in a relationship. She would hate him, and then he'd be all mine again.

It was the day before Thanksgiving. I waited until 6 p.m. and saw her walk out of their office building, alone. *Thank God.* I followed her onto the train, and she exited at 14th St to take the L train. *Okay, good. The L goes to Williamsburg; she's going home.* I quietly stalked her in the crowd as she walked toward McCarren Park. She entered a building right in front of it, and I stood beside it after she walked in, figuring out what to do next. That's when I felt his hand grip my arm.

"Jackie, what are you doing here?" His voice was menacing and low, but somehow it wasn't as sinister as I knew it could be.

I began to tremble. How was I going to explain myself? Was he stalking her too?

"I...I just wanted to talk to her," I fumbled out, facing my beautiful Michael. He was in his work clothes with a black peacoat on, his hair perfectly styled with just a stubble of facial hair. His dark gray eyes bore into mine, but they softened slightly.

"No." He smiled mockingly and shook his head. "No, baby. You can't talk to her."

I pulled away from his grip. "You can't stop me from talking to her, Michael." My voice was loud and unwavering, the lump in my throat threatening to make me start sobbing.

Michael searched my face, contemplating his next move.

"What do you need so you won't talk to her?" *Is he bargaining with me?* "How much?"

I began to cry. "I don't want money, Michael. I want you!" I huffed out.

## THEN

He sighed with frustration. "Do you want me to call the police again? Have them charge you for stalking and threatening me and my girlfriend?"

I immediately shook my head. "No, please. I just need you, Michael. I need you, Daddy." Tears streamed down my face.

He sighed again, rolling his eyes. "Of course you do, Jackie. Do you know how pathetic you sound?"

My hand trembled in my coat pocket, gripping my phone. An idea suddenly struck me.

"Okay. Money. I want money." I pulled my phone out of my pocket, quickly opening the wallet app to request money.

Michael shook his head. "You're a fucking leech, do you know that?" He pulled out his phone and began tapping the screen.

I discreetly opened the voice memos app and started recording, then went back to the wallet app.

"How much?" He looked up at me with contempt.

"How much do you think it's worth for me to shut my mouth? To not tell her everything?" I raised my eyebrows at him, trying to appear brave, but my heart was racing.

His eye twitched. "Ten grand?"

I smiled. "How about ten grand for every fucking scar you've given me? I think that would put you at like...a million?"

Michael clenched his jaw. "You do not expect me to just give you a million dollars, Jackie. You deserved those fucking scars for trying to leave me."

"And now? Now you want me to leave you?" I couldn't believe I was getting this all on audio.

"I want you to leave me alone. I will come to you and use you when I see fit."

I scoffed. "Like the other night? Just fucking me and

discarding me like trash?"

He smiled. "Exactly, baby. You know you're fucking trash."

My heart raced with anger and excitement. I smiled back as I lifted my phone and stopped the recording. Michael's eyes widened when he realized what I had done. I quickly put the phone back in my pocket for safety.

"Here's the plan, Michael," I started, my voice quiet and shaky. "You have a week to call it off with her unless you want me to show this to her."

"And then what?" he hissed.

"And then you're all mine again."

He shook his head. "You won't fucking show her that, Jackie. Give me your phone."

I looked around at the crowded park across the street and then back at him. I was safe in public, so I could be brave. "No. And I will."

"I'm going with her to her parents' house tonight, Jackie. You don't expect me to just call it off with her. She's not just a fucking plaything like you are."

My heart stung at his words. "Figure it out, Michael." I couldn't believe he was buying it; I wasn't even sure if I believed myself. He could grab me and carry me off into an alley, and no one would really bat an eye. "And as soon as you get back, I want you at my apartment, and I want you to be my Daddy again." My voice was weakening.

I could tell he was thinking of some sort of plan. I knew this was going to end badly.

"Okay, baby. Don't do anything stupid while I'm gone, okay?" I melted at his words.

I nodded. "Okay, Daddy."

# Now

If you would have told me months ago that I'd be suspended in the air, tied up and exposed for the most amazing man in the world, I wouldn't have believed you. But there I was, still in the frog tie with my hands above me, hanging from a bar on the ceiling. Elliott watched me intently as he pulled toys out from his closet, smiling cleverly at me. My legs were wide open and his cum was still leaking from each of my holes.

"Look at my beautiful girl," he mused as he walked towards me with a magic wand in his hand; I had never used one before, but I heard they were intense.

The toy began to buzz loudly as he turned it on. My heart raced as he inched closer to me, his cock growing hard again.

"I can't wait to make you come until you're begging for me to stop." He smiled, grabbing hold of my thigh.

My dominant Elliott was the hottest thing I'd ever seen.

He put the powerful wand to my clit and my pussy immediately began to seize. The vibration was so intense that I tried to close my legs, but they were spread open, unable to budge. I came harder than I ever had before—and liquid began to gush out of me as I screamed out with pleasure. I had never squirted before and I laughed with surprise once I calmed down. Elliott's eyes were widened with a smile, the evidence of my intense orgasm dripping down his body.

"Holy shit," I said, bewildered.

Elliott licked his lips slowly and shook his head with a tsk.

"What did I say about that mouth, baby?" He set down the wand before he took a riding crop and held the leather tip to his palm; I knew what was coming for my dirty mouth.

I smiled with anticipation. Elliott circled around me and quickly tapped my ass with the crop, the feeling more pleasurable than painful, but it still made me jump and gasp. He came back around in front of me, his eyes clouded with desire and something I hadn't seen from him before. Darkness? It made my heart skip a beat, but somehow I wasn't afraid.

He quickly tapped me on the inside of my thigh, startling me again.

"Oh, baby. You're so reactive to me. You are so fun to play with, my sweet girl," he marveled.

My heart stung at his words: *my sweet girl*. Only Michael had called me that before.

"Daddy, you make me feel so good. More, *please*," I begged.

He chuckled as he dropped the riding crop and brought me closer to him. He got down on his knees and pressed his tongue lightly against my clit, teasing me as he continued to barely flick the sensitive spot. He gripped my thighs with both of his hands as he buried his face in my pussy, now lapping around and seeming determined to make me come again. It didn't take long for him to accomplish it—I came hard, my whole body shaking as I lifted my thighs, trying to chase more.

"Mmm, baby. You taste so good; I can't get enough," he murmured into my pussy, the vibration from his lips inching me closer to another orgasm.

He suddenly stood up, letting go of me, making me groan

with the need for another orgasm. I watched as he grabbed the wand and began to stroke himself. He walked behind me, doing something with the rope that held me from above. *Oh—he's lowering me.* I heard the wand turn on as he appeared in front of me, still stroking himself.

"Your pussy is just too good. I need to fuck you and make you come again." With that, he put the wand to my clit and thrust himself inside of me at the same time. I screamed out with satisfaction, knowing my throbbing clit was going to make me clench around Elliott's cock quickly. I was right—I came for what seemed like the hundredth time, but I was still needing more; I couldn't get enough of Elliott either.

He began to thrust faster, grunting wildly with primal moans that drove me crazy. I could tell he was coming, and knowing that, I came again, my whole body shaking wildly, my pussy satisfied. And I was fucking exhausted.

Elliott quickly untied me, carried me to the bathtub, and sat me down on the edge as he ran a warm bath.

"How was that? How are you feeling, baby?" he asked gently as he sat down next to me, then gently pressed his lips to my shoulder.

I sighed happily with a smile. "Amazing. It was perfect, Daddy. So fucking perfect." I may have added in the *fuck* to see if Elliott would want to punish me.

He shook his head and eyed me with a smile. "Such a dirty fucking mouth. I love it." Then he pressed his lips fervently against mine, holding my cheek and pulling me closer. Somehow, we ended up fucking again as he bent me over the bathroom counter, and then he gently washed me in the tub, providing me with the aftercare I needed—and deserved.

\* \* \*

I slept soundly that night. For once, my thoughts weren't racing with worries about the future because I knew what it held: a life with Elliott, who would always take care of me. And I wanted to take care of him too.

However, that feeling didn't last long.

I was awoken by my phone vibrating violently on the nightstand. I grabbed it, and my heart dropped—it was from an unknown number. I glanced at the clock on Elliott's nightstand: it read 2:30 a.m. *What. The. Fuck.* I almost began to hyperventilate until Elliott flicked on his lamp and quickly sat up.

"What's wrong? What is it?"

"I think..." I began with shaky breath. "I think it's Michael."

The call went to voicemail, but then a text popped up from a number I didn't recognize. My heart dropped to my stomach, and bile rose in my throat. It was a picture of me and Elliott, walking hand in hand into his house. It had been taken a few hours earlier when we had just gotten home, seemingly from across the street.

"Oh my God...it's him," I muttered, somehow out of breath.

"God fucking damnit," Elliott hissed as he looked over my shoulder at the picture. He threw the blankets off and stood up. "Enough is enough." He turned on the light in his closet and began rifling through things.

I didn't pay any attention; my mind raced over the fact that Michael was watching us. He was in LA. And he was taunting me. What was he trying to do? What was he *going* to do? I gasped when Elliott walked out of the closet with a gun in his hand, eyeing me with the intensity and fierceness I had seen earlier.

"Holy shit, Elliott! What are you doing?" I jumped out of bed, shaking on my unsteady feet.

"I'm stopping Michael. I don't fucking care. If he's here, I'm going to fucking kill him." He walked out of the room and stomped down the hallway, putting the gun into the waistband of his gray joggers. I followed, my heart pounding out of my chest, my palms sweaty and shaky. Elliott flung the front door open and stood on the steps, looking around as if Michael would just be standing there, waiting for us.

"Elliott, please, come inside," I begged him. I was afraid Michael was actually out there, set up with a rifle, ready to shoot anyone who stepped outside.

"Stop being a fucking coward!" Elliott yelled into the darkness.

I heard myself breathing rapidly as I waited for a response, poking my head out the door while hiding behind the wall.

"Please, Elliott. Come inside!" I whispered loudly.

Elliott looked around for another moment before marching back inside, closing the door behind us, and locking it. His chest heaved up and down quickly, and his eyes were wide with anger.

"Jacqueline, I need to tell you something." He took my hand and pulled me into the kitchen, flicking on the light.

We stood on the cold tile as his expression shifted from anger to something else I hadn't seen before: fear. He licked his lips and gulped, taking my other hand and holding both of them gently, shaking his head.

"Baby, I need you to believe me. I need you to know that I love you, that I genuinely love you, and I never thought this would happen." His breath was shaky—he seemed nervous to continue.

"What?" I asked, confused.

He shook his head again. "Michael hired me to follow you."

My whole world began to spin, swirling dizzily around me. I gripped the nearest surface for support, feeling lightheaded and on the brink of losing consciousness. The taste of bile surged in my throat again, threatening to overwhelm me.

"What?" I didn't believe him—he must have been joking. But why would he joke about something so terrible?

"I didn't know he had done those things to you. He called me because I work as a private investigator on the side. I have my license and everything. I boarded that flight from New York to LA with the intention of only following you to see what you were up to. I never intended to fall in love with you. I had no idea what he did, baby. I need you to believe me."

Tears welled in his eyes, and my knees buckled from underneath me. I landed straight on my ass and began to hyperventilate. *This can't be happening. This isn't true. This can't be fucking true.* Elliott leaned down and took my hands again, now too close for comfort.

"No, no, no." I shook my head, pulling my hands away, sobbing uncontrollably.

"Please, baby. Everything about us is real. I'm real, everything you know about me is real, and you're the best thing that's ever happened to me."

It sounded like he was speaking to me from inside a tunnel. My heart felt like it was getting squeezed and crushed by a hydraulic press. How did this happen? He had lied to me this whole time. He knew Michael—he was fucking *hired* by him. To stalk me! *Oh my God...*

I immediately stood up, completely ignoring anything else

Elliott was saying. I could never, ever trust him again. How could I? He was associated with the devil himself. How could he *not* know? My legs began to move quickly, and I ran out the front door, barefoot in only a big T-shirt and underwear. Elliott called out for me but I ran faster down the hill of his street. If Michael was watching, he'd pick me up and kill me, I just knew it. *Fine, just fucking kill me. I don't have anything left in me to fight anymore. I don't have* anyone *anymore.*

"Please, Jacqueline!"

Elliott was right behind me; he quickly caught up with me and wrapped his arms around me from behind. I began to scream and kick as he lifted my feet off the ground, whispering in my ear, but I was too busy freaking the fuck out. He held onto me tight until I wore myself out—then I slumped into his arms and began to sob again. My tears fell onto his big forearms that held me tight.

"Why?" I asked between hiccuped sobs.

"If I let you go, please don't run, baby. We need to talk, but not out in the middle of the street, especially if he's around." His voice was gentle and I felt his hot breath against my ear.

I began to laugh. All of this was absolutely absurd to me.

"You know, maybe that wouldn't be so bad anymore. You and your best friend can fucking take turns torturing me."

Elliott quickly let me go. I didn't bother to move; I just stood there catching my breath, still shaking from my sobs.

"You really think I'd hurt you?" He sounded devastated. But so was I.

"No, but I also didn't think you were fucking in cahoots with Michael, but here we are."

We were both still standing in the street, my back against Elliott's chest. He gently put his hands on my shoulders and I flinched; it broke my heart.

"I swear to God, Jacqueline. If I had known what he did to you, I would have fucking killed him."

My heart was crushed. So what if what he was saying was true? He still kept a huge secret from me—what if he had more that he wasn't revealing about himself?

"I need to leave. I can't stay with you right now." My voice wavered, tears still streaming down my face.

Elliott let go of my shoulders and gently turned me around. I couldn't look up at him; I was afraid that I wouldn't leave if I looked into his bright blue, kind eyes. That's how he fooled me before.

"Take my car. Go where you need to go," he said gently.

I immediately shook my head. "No. I'll get an Uber." I stepped aside to move past him and walk back up the hill.

"Baby, you'll be safe here with me," he said, close behind me.

"You're not allowed to call me baby anymore, Elliott." It pained me to say those words aloud.

"Please, Jacqueline. I don't want you to leave. I want to talk about this."

I kept silent as we walked up the steep hill. I was out of breath and shaking from the cold and emotional turmoil that ran through my body.

We walked into the house and I stormed into the room, grabbed my phone from the nightstand, pulled some pants on, and stuffed as many things as I could into a small bag. My only thought was to get the hell out of there as soon as I could. Elliott followed me to the front door and closed it with his palm as soon as I tried to open it.

I turned and glared at him. "Move."

## NOW

He clenched his jaw. "Jacqueline. Please. Who knows where Michael is? What if he follows you?" His eyes were soft despite the way he growled at me.

"I'll take my chances. Now fucking move." My heart raced as I locked eyes with him, refusing to look away.

He shook his head but removed his hand from the door and stepped back. I quickly opened the door and pulled up the Uber app, requesting a ride to the nearest hotel. A car was five minutes away. I sat halfway down the stairs that led to the street; I could feel Elliott standing at the open door, watching me.

"I love you, Jacqueline. Please...please don't leave." His voice cracked with his last two words.

I put my face in my hands and shook my head.

"Please, Elliott. Please leave me alone."

I don't know why I felt a pang of disappointment when I heard the door gently close behind me. The soft click echoed in the hollow space of my heart, amplifying the emptiness inside. I began to sob, tears streaming down my face as I made my way to the waiting Uber. As I slid into the back seat, the weight of my shattered emotions pressed down on me, leaving me feeling completely and utterly broken.

# Then

I obsessively checked Hana's Instagram while she and Michael were away. She never posted anything, but she was tagged by someone named Emily; her last name was also Miller, so I assumed they were related. There were selfies of the two, but nothing Michael related. She was so beautiful and thin with amazing cheekbones. No wonder he didn't want me anymore when he could have her.

The night after Thanksgiving, I sat in my room and mindlessly skimmed through a book. My brain was far too distracted to read the words. And then I received a text from him: **Unlock your door. Wait for me in your bedroom on your knees.**

My heart raced in my chest as I smiled down at my phone. Thank God my roommate wasn't home; Michael had never actually been in my apartment, so I was curious if he was going to search around the place to look for me.

**Yes, Daddy.**

I ran to the front door, unlocked it, and then ran back to my room. I got on my knees with a smile on my face. I must have waited ten minutes until my front door creaked open. I heard his footsteps slowly approach my room and I bit my lip as my chest quickly heaved up and down. Instinctively, my eyes went to the floor as he walked in. My bedroom door shut behind him.

He chuckled faintly. "Sweet Jackie. All ready for me."

I smiled at the floor. "Yes, Daddy."

He crept closer to me, his brown oxfords stopping right in front of my knees.

"Stand up. Eyes down."

I quickly stood on wobbly legs. Now that Michael was in front of me, all alone, fear struck through my chest. Was he going to punish me?

He slowly circled me, just as he did the first night we met. He stopped behind me and took my wrists, holding them together with one hand. He pulled me a step back and then shoved me down into the bed, face first. He was quiet—too quiet.

Suddenly, he was pulling down my jeans and panties in one quick motion. I gasped as he began to softly caress my ass; I let out a scream as he slapped it hard with his hand.

"Sweet Jackie. Why have you been so naughty, hm?" His voice was quiet, as if he feared being heard.

"Because I've missed you, Daddy. I told you I'd never stop loving you," I whispered as a hot tear fell down my cheek.

He sighed. "That you did. So fucking persistent." He sounded annoyed, but he began to graze my ass again.

"No one will ever love you the way that I do, Daddy. I'm yours, forever. I'll never leave." My voice was strained as Michael took my wrists and held them down against the small of my back.

"Yeah, I'm starting to fucking notice that, Jackie." There was contempt clear in his voice.

I heard his zipper being pulled down; my pussy began to throb for him.

"I haven't used my belt on you yet, have I?" It was eerie how calm and even his voice was.

A lump formed in my throat and fear rose in my chest. "No," I whispered.

He slapped hard down onto my ass.

"No, Daddy. You haven't," I corrected myself.

That's when he replaced his hand with his belt—a hard, quick, stinging pain seared on my ass and made me cry out with pain. Michael held my wrists tighter as he whacked me again, this time harder; the pain was unbearable but I needed to be his good girl and be quiet to please him. I began to sob as he struck me a third and fourth time.

"Sweet fucking Jackie. Do you want Daddy to fuck you?" He no longer sounded angry—in fact, he sounded heated and turned on as he dropped his belt to the floor.

"Yes, please, Daddy," I cried, my tears unable to stop.

He kept a firm grip on my wrists as he quickly thrust himself inside of me. He grabbed my hair with his free hand and tugged it back hard, sending more searing pain through me.

"You don't deserve to come. Wanna know why, Jackie?" His lips traced my ear as he fucked me hard and deep.

He didn't wait for me to answer.

"Because like I said: you're fucking trash; you're just a cum dumpster and I'll always use you how I please."

His words pricked deep down in my chest.

He grunted hard as he came inside of me, his cum quickly spilling out of me. He pulled out and grabbed his belt off the floor; I began to squirm as he wrapped the leather around my wrists, locking my arms in place behind my back. I finally looked back at him; just as he let go of me, his eyes scanned my room in search of something.

"What are you doing?" I cried as he walked around my room, inching closer to my phone on the nightstand, almost camouflaged atop a black book.

I realized he found it as he smiled to himself and headed straight for it. I knew what he was gonna do—he was going to erase evidence of his confession.

"Please, don't," I begged, wobbling as I stood up to face him, my hands still bound behind my back.

He ignored me as he tapped something into my phone. He guessed my password right away: his birthday.

"Fucking obsessed with me, aren't you?" He quickly glanced up at me with disdain, then looked back down at my phone.

"Michael," I cried, sitting on the bed, losing hope.

He continued to ignore me as he erased the voice note. Of course, I was stupid enough to not back it up anywhere, so I knew it was gone; I lost the upper hand. My head slumped down in front of me as he tossed the phone next to me on the bed.

"I can tell by how defeated you look that that was the only copy," he said, his voice smug and triumphant.

I looked up just as he pulled his zipper up and buttoned his jeans.

I shook my head at him, feeling hopeless and shattered. "Now what?"

He raised his eyebrows at me as if he were surprised.

"Now what?" He laughed, mocking me again. "Now nothing. Now you need to leave me and Hana the fuck alone."

I expected that answer but it didn't stop me from continuing to sob. *This is it. I'm losing him.*

"Won't you still come see me…when you want to?" I hated how pathetic and desperate I sounded.

He scoffed and shook his head, heading for the door. Without looking back, he said, "Sure, Jackie. When I feel like beating the shit out of someone, you'll be the first one I call."

# Now

I turned my phone off once I made it safely into the hotel only a few minutes away from Elliott's house. I ran a hot bath and soaked in the tub, my salty tears mixing with the clean water.

Michael *hired* Elliott. Michael gave Elliott money to *watch* me like a fucking spy. I felt like I didn't even know who he was anymore. He was a private investigator on the side? *What the fuck?* Did he go to New York *just* to follow me? Was Kate real? Was any of it real? He said it was but how was I going to believe someone who fucking followed me and lied about it? His charming smile, his persistent attempts to talk to me on the plane, giving me his card—it was all just a ploy to get closer to me, wasn't it? Pretending to be such a fucking gentleman. But...he *was* a gentleman. He made me feel safe and loved. But how could I ever forgive him for this? How could I ever trust him again? He knew my past and was too fucking selfish to tell me the truth. He got me into this deep love affair by fucking lying to me.

And Michael—Michael knew exactly where I was. He was in LA, taking pictures of me and Elliott. Did he know where I worked too? Did he know where I was while I stayed at the hostel? Of course he did. I'm sure Elliott told him. And then Elliott coaxed me into moving in with him.

*Fuck.*

I fell asleep in the bathtub. I woke up gasping, the cold water sloshing around as I quickly sat up, remembering where I was and the nightmare that had followed me across the country. Sunlight shone through the window in the hotel room. *Awesome, almost accidentally drowning? I'm doing fucking great.*

I turned my phone on and a flood of texts came through, all from Elliott.

**Jacqueline, once you've slept on it, please come back.**

**I am not "in cahoots" with Michael, baby. I never was.**

**I love you. Everything between us has been real. I haven't lied to you about anything, baby.**

**I'm so sorry I've hurt you. I never wanted this to happen. I didn't expect to fall in love with you. The only thing Michael did was hire me. I didn't know anything else, I swear.**

**Good morning. Please call me. I love you.**

My finger hovered over the message box. I wanted to reach out to him; I missed him so fucking much. But did he deserve my time? Did he deserve the opportunity to explain himself? Before I could change my mind, I turned my phone off again. Realizing I had to work in just a couple hours, I showered, got dressed, and took an Uber to work.

I was thankful that I had work to keep my mind occupied. Although there was a dull ache deep in my chest, the restaurant was busy enough to keep my thoughts focused on what was happening right in front of me.

There was only an hour until closing. Things were just starting to slow down when our host eyed me and tilted his head toward the corner of the restaurant, indicating we had a new diner in my area.

I pulled out the tablet we used to take orders and stopped in my tracks when I looked up and realized who was sitting there, smiling at me smugly: Michael. Fucking. Barnes. I was sure I was about to have a heart attack; my throat constricted, my chest tightened, and my whole body buzzed with fear. I don't know how my legs started to move towards him, but somehow, I got closer as my heart pounded against my lungs.

"Hello, sweet Jackie." His deep voice and Irish accent still did things to me, and I hated myself for it.

"What are you doing here?" My weak voice sounded so foreign to me in this setting, where bubbly Jackie was front and center.

Michael smiled and lifted his brows, eyeing me up and down.

"You look well. Have you lost weight? Or gained? I can't tell. Something is different though."

Of course, he would immediately try to belittle me and my appearance. He looked exactly the same, except for the strands of gray in his beard and hair. He looked so fucking hot, and I hated myself for thinking it.

"Are you here to eat or to ask me my fucking weight?" I wasn't surprised at my courage peeking through—we were in public, at my workplace, where he couldn't do anything to me.

He laughed, and despite my best efforts, my insides melted. His laughter sent a shiver down my spine, and my heart stung at how much I still reacted to him. The sight of him made my pulse quicken and heat soar through my body.

"Neither," he said, his eyes locking onto mine with a familiar intensity. "I'm here to take back what's mine."

*No.*

I laughed nervously. "What, can't find any other of your victims? Didn't get the help from your private investigator? Or does he just focus on one person at a time?"

He looked surprised. "He told you."

Tears pricked my eyes. "Of course he told me."

Now Michael smiled again. "Much to your dismay, hm? I'm surprised the lad even took any interest in you."

*That's* what pushed my anger over the edge. "And why do *you* still have any interest in me, Michael?"

He put his elbows on the table and leaned forward. "Out of all the women I've ever been with, you're the one who was the most submissive, the easiest to control, the easiest to manipulate." He chuckled to himself and I stood there frozen, trying to grasp my reality. "I'll never find anyone as fucking weak as you, sweet Jackie. That's why you're perfect for me."

I hated myself. I hated the way all of his other words were thrown out the window because of his last declaration. My mind threw all logic out the window. My years of therapy were instantly fizzled away like magic. All I had wanted for so long was to be his. And now he was admitting to me that he still wanted me.

"*There's* that spark in your eye, sweet Jackie. I know you still want me." He looked so pleased with himself—and with *me.* "After work, you're coming back to my hotel. And you will be my pet, baby. You will be my fucking puppet all over again."

I heard dishes clanking together in the background, pulling me out of his trance. I quickly shook my head. "No."

He looked amused as he sat back in his seat and raised his eyebrows. "No?"

"No," I repeated. "I am *not* yours anymore, Michael."

He rolled his eyes. "Okay, Jackie. If I bent you over my knee right here, right now, I know you'd be soaking wet for me."

He wasn't wrong. But just because my body wanted him didn't mean *I* wanted him.

"Everything okay here, Jackie?" My co-worker's voice startled me as I whipped my head back in her direction.

"Yeah uh, actually...could you take this one? I need to leave. It's an emergency, Meg. I'll tell Lauren."

My poor co-worker nodded at me sympathetically. "Of course, babe. Go ahead. I got this."

I didn't even bother to look back at Michael; all I knew was that I needed to get out of there. *Immediately.*

I went into the break room to gather my belongings and turned my phone on. There were more texts from Elliott, but I didn't read them; instead, I called him. He answered right away.

"Jacqueline," he breathed, sounding relieved. "I've been so fucking worried."

"Michael is here," I blurted out. "He's at my work. Please come get me. Please come now." The lump in my throat finally took over, and I began to bawl, not even realizing my whole body was shaking until I sat down.

"Jesus Christ. I'm on my way. Are you inside? Are you safe?" I heard keys banging together as if he were running to his car.

"Yes, I'm in the break room. We don't close for another hour," I explained through my tears.

"Stay on the line with me, baby." I heard his car start and an engine revving, tires screeching.

"Please tell me you didn't know. Please tell me you really love me, Elliott. Please." I put my knees up to my chest and hugged them with one arm while the other held my phone to my ear.

"Yes, baby, I love you. I love you more than anything. I swear to God I had no idea what he did to you." His voice was panicked and it scared me; hearing him unraveled was unnerving.

His words didn't stop the ache in my chest, the utter devastation and betrayal I felt. But I loved Elliott—*that* I knew. And I needed him, especially now. If he wasn't in my life, I would already be bent over Michael's knee.

"I love you, Elliott. I'm scared," I admitted.

I was not only scared of Michael but also of how much I already loved Elliott and how my heart was already broken by both of them.

"I'm not gonna let anything happen to you, baby. I'm right here. I will be there in just a few minutes, okay?"

Meg walked in and interrupted my thoughts as she bent down and put her hand to my shoulder. "Babe, you okay?"

I shook my head. "No. That man out there—he's my ex. He's my abusive fucking ex," I cried to her.

She gasped. "Oh God, Jackie. Are you okay? He fucking bolted right after you walked away."

Relief suddenly flooded my entire body.

"Oh, thank God." I sighed.

"I'll make sure Lauren bans him. Fucking loser," Meg huffed.

"Thanks. I'm on the phone with my boyfriend. He's picking me up now," I explained.

*My boyfriend.*

"Good," Meg said as she stood up. "I'll keep an eye out." She patted my shoulder and walked out.

"Elliott?" I said into the phone.

"I'm here, baby." He was starting to sound relieved. "I'm about five minutes away."

I nodded and my head pounded with a sudden headache.

"Okay. Call me when you're here. I need to gather my thoughts." I hung up.

I needed to gather all the facts—I needed to *think.* This is

## NOW

what I knew: Michael hired Elliott to see what I was up to. Was he still in prison then? And when exactly did he get out? Elliott found out that I was boarding a plane to LA—how? And then he got the seat directly next to me. He befriended and disarmed me with his smile and gentleness. He gave me his card, hoping I'd call him. But he knew my number anyway, didn't he? He had to have known. Then Michael began harassing me again—*and* Elliott? When did Elliott tell him to fuck off? Or did he ever? So many questions ran through my head as my phone buzzed in my hand.

Elliott walked through the back to come get me. He took my hand without saying a word; his eyes were concerned and focused as he led me to his car, opened the door for me, and then hopped in next to me. He sped off onto Beverly Blvd and reached over to take my hand.

"Take me to my hotel. I can't be at your house right now," I said quietly, not moving my hand away from his, but looking out the window.

"Please let me stay with you. Jacqueline, I need to protect you. I need to figure out what Michael is trying to do," he responded sternly.

I looked over at him and shook my head. His worried eyes met mine as we stopped at a red light.

"He's trying to get me back. He said he was here to take back what's his."

Elliott's eyebrows lifted as he scoffed. "Is that what he said? That motherfucker," he muttered through gritted teeth.

The light turned green.

"I think he's right, Elliott," I murmured, feeling like I was punched in the gut. "I think I am his. I wanted to go with him tonight, but I snapped out of it. But deep down, I wanted to go."

*Why am I telling him this?*

Elliott only shook his head and clenched his jaw. My gaze kept steadily on him.

"Baby, he put you through so much. He fucked with your mind. I'm sure seeing him again stirred up all kinds of feelings but I know you would never get back with him; you're stronger than that now."

I rolled my eyes. He didn't know me at all. I wasn't strong; I would always be weak, naive, sweet Jackie.

"I'm at the Hollywood Hotel, just before your house," I said, ignoring him.

He kept quiet as we continued to drive east.

"Can we talk?" His voice sounded sad and defeated.

"About you working with Michael?" I asked, the anger from earlier bubbling back into my chest.

He sighed heavily. "Will you let me explain?"

I shrugged and crossed my arms as I looked out the window.

"I got a call from him a few days before we met on the plane," he began, and I resisted every urge to yell that he stalked me onto the plane. "He told me that he wanted to know what an ex-girlfriend was up to. I figured he just wanted to reconnect with an old flame and see if she was involved with anyone. So I looked into you—the very basics. I knew your name, where you lived in New York, where you worked. I spoke with some of your old co-workers and they told me you were moving to LA. I figured out what flight you were taking and got the seat next to you. All I planned to do was make friendly conversation, but you seemed to hate me from the beginning, which surprised me since I didn't realize why. I planned to give Michael the simple information I gathered—that you had moved to LA. And I gave you my card because I actually wanted to get to know you; it wasn't under the guise of trying to gather information on you. And then...then I instantly fell in love with you. And when I found out what he did to you, I told him I wasn't going to work for him and gave him his money back. He started harassing you, and I figured out that he blocked me when I tried to confront him. Then he began harassing both of us and...and now here we are."

I blinked back tears as I continued to look out the window, unable to face him. I wanted to reach over and tell him I was scared, that he was the only person in the world who made me feel safe, even after what I had learned. I wanted to tell him that I loved him so fucking much and that he made me feel so loved and wanted. But instead, I stewed in my anger and fear, knowing that my instincts had led me down the wrong path over and over again.

Elliott kept quiet as we approached my hotel. He quickly got out and opened my door for me, then took my hand; I gave in and held onto his. I stopped before we entered the lobby, looking up at him and shaking my head.

"Please. I need some time. You're close; if anything happens, I'll call you right away."

He looked like he was about to cry, or worse...that he was scared.

"At least let me walk you to your room," he pleaded.

I shook my head again. "You need a card to get in every door. It's safe. I'll be fine." *What great famous last words.*

Elliott gulped and then softly squeezed my hand. "I love you, Jacqueline."

I nodded. "I know." *I love you too.* I let go of his hand, swiped my card for the lobby door, and quickly walked in, tears streaming down my face.

I sluggishly walked into the elevator, went up to my floor, and swiped the key to my room.

Heat rose to my cheeks and fear consumed my body once I shut the door behind me and realized I wasn't alone. He sat on the lone arm chair beside the bed with a devious glare and a smile on his face.

"Hello, sweet Jackie."

# Then

Months went by with radio silence from Michael. I had given up on him, only because I had no other choice. I tried to blackmail him and failed miserably. I tried to make him love me but I couldn't. I continued to watch him and Hana from afar and drank myself into oblivion. I watched as they moved into a fancy condo in Chelsea. I saw the ring on Hana's finger as they went out on dates. I watched as they met at Battery Park during lunch hour, making out in front of everyone as they sat on a bench in the tree-lined park. Michael would glance over his shoulder and glare at me, then wrap his arm snugly around Hana. I was crushed; I was never going to get him back, and I wanted to die. I had nothing; I had no one. I was far too fucked up to be able to continue my life. I would never be happy, not without him.

But one cold February night, as I sat on the floor of my dimly lit room, tipping back a 40 oz bottle and feeling the burn of the alcohol down my throat, my phone began to buzz. My heart nearly stopped when I saw who was calling. A wave of nausea hit me, and I almost puked. With trembling hands, I instantly answered.

"Michael?" My voice cracked.

"Sweet Jackie." His voice was chipper, far from his usual

tone; I figured he was drunk. "What's my baby doing?"

My heart pounded as tears filled my eyes. "I'm—I'm not doing anything. Why are you calling me?" I was too confused to understand what was happening.

Michael laughed on the other end. "Come over, baby. Please. I want to see you. I've got a new place in Williamsburg."

My mouth flew wide open. I had been dreaming of this day for months. He sounded so normal, so unlike his usual cruel, dominant self. I didn't know how to react.

"Okay. Do you want me over right now?" I asked hesitantly.

He chuckled again. "Yes, sweet Jackie. Come now. I'm texting you my address." He hung up.

I received his address not long after. He was only a couple of short train rides away. I quickly got into the shower, threw on some clothes, and headed for the train. Twenty minutes later, I was standing at his front door, watching my shaky fist carefully knock. Michael quickly opened the door, and my heart dropped; he stood there wearing nothing but boxer briefs with his hard cock bulging underneath. His fucking abs and arms and thick, muscled thighs made my mouth water. And oddly enough, he was smiling at me.

"Sweet Jackie. Come in, baby." He held the door open and gestured for me to come in.

I looked around his fancy apartment. There were floor-to-ceiling windows in the two-story space, offering stunning views of Manhattan across the river. But I didn't have much time to take it in; I heard the door close behind me, and Michael was quickly standing behind me, slipping his hands up the front of my shirt after shrugging off my jacket. I could smell the alcohol on him, but I already knew he had been drinking.

"Mmm, your nice, big, perky tits," he whispered in my ear,

then pressed his lips to my neck.

My heart began to stomp furiously in my chest, his touch instantly making me wet between my thighs. I closed my eyes and basked in his gentle touch. Had I finally died and this was my reward?

"Does my good girl want Daddy's cock?" His voice was soothing as he pressed his lips to my shoulder, pressing his hard cock against my ass.

"Yes, please, Daddy," I moaned as goosebumps prickled my body.

Michael suddenly pulled both of my arms behind me, holding my wrists in place with one hand. I watched as he pulled rope out of the console table in the hallway where we stood. I stood there patiently as he tied my wrists together, then ripped my thin T-shirt apart, exposing my breasts to the cold air. He hooked his thumbs into my jeans at each hip and quickly pulled them down along with my underwear. I stepped out of them and waited for his next move.

"On your knees, sweet Jackie. Eyes on the floor."

I smiled as I dropped down to my knees and kept my eyes pointed down at the floor in front of me. Michael slowly walked in my view and I heard the motions of him jerking off.

"God, look at my sweet Jackie, with my name carved all over you. My property. Such a beautiful fucking sight to see," he gruffed. "You haven't shown anyone else, have you?" It was more of a statement than a question.

I quickly shook my head. "No, Daddy."

"Why not?"

I blinked down at the floor. "Because I love you, Daddy. I only want you."

He laughed loudly. "So fucking desperate. My pretty, sweet

Jackie. How did you become so fucking weak?"

Tears began welling in my eyes. I didn't know how to answer, or if he even wanted me to.

"Doesn't matter. All that matters is that you belong to me. You'd do anything for me, wouldn't you?" His voice was booming and becoming more and more sinister as he spoke.

My tears began to stream down my face. "Yes, Daddy."

Michael put his hand to the back of my head and tugged on my hair, forcing me to look up at him; his eyes were dark and angry.

"You're mine, Jackie. All. Fucking. Mine. Do you understand?"

Amidst the suffocating fear, there was a strange, twisted hope settling into my chest. "Yes, Daddy. I understand."

He quickly slapped me hard across the cheek and the pain made me scream out.

His words spit out at me. "You are bound to me. You will always be mine. You will do as I say and you will be my fucking pet until you die."

I began to sob; I didn't know why he was so angry when I was being so compliant. All I could do was nod and say, "Yes, Daddy."

"All of you fucking women are the same, do you know that? Such weak, pathetic pieces of shit."

He walked around me and pushed me down onto the floor with his foot, face first; I had nothing to stop my fall with my arms being bound as my head hit the floor with a bang. Michael lifted up my hips and my knees steadied on the floor, and I screamed as his hard cock pushed deep inside of me.

"So fucking wet, my sweet Jackie. Such a fucking whore," he spit out, digging his nails into the flesh of my hips as he thrust quickly in and out of me.

I lost count of the amount of times he slapped down hard on my ass. He wasn't just tapping me—he was beating me. He was taking out whatever pent up anger he had on me. All I could think was that Hana had left him; she found out who he really was and she left him. I hated that I was relieved, that I had him to myself again.

Michael grabbed me by the hair and lifted me up against his chest, putting his hand to my throat with his other hand and squeezing tight—so tight that I quickly passed out with him still inside of me, fucking me hard.

I woke up with my arms and legs tied to his bed. I was lightheaded, and my throat felt bruised. It was dark, and I couldn't see anything except for a faint light in another room. In the distance, I heard the sound of running water. The water suddenly stopped, and a moment later, Michael walked out, dripping wet, eyeing me with a sinister smile.

"Sweet Jackie. You've revived. Are you ready for more?"

My throat ached as I whispered, "Yes, Daddy."

I would do anything to please him, to make him happy, just so I could be his again.

He laughed as he walked over to his dresser and grabbed something small. It was so dark that I couldn't see what it was. He slowly walked to his bedside table and turned on the lamp, revealing what was in his hand—a sharp knife. *No...oh God, not again.*

"I thought it might be more fun to fuck you while I carve my name into you again. Perhaps your arms this time?" He spoke so lightly, as if he were talking about the weather, as he hopped on top of me, straddling me.

"Please, no, Daddy," I cried, tugging on my bound arms and

legs.

"No?" He raised his eyebrows angrily. "You don't get to say no, sweet Jackie. I own you and your body. I will do as I please."

I began to cry as he turned around and loosened the rope around my ankles. I didn't bother to try to fight—it would just anger him more. He made another elaborate knot with my ankles tied to my thighs so I was spread open for him, but unable to move. He lifted my hips up and thrust himself inside of me, holding onto the knife as he smiled down at me, grabbing my breast with his free hand. He quickly pulled out of me and forced himself in my ass, the lubrication from my pussy enough to slide himself inside, but it still hurt. He then held the knife up in his right hand, stilled his hips, and lifted up his left arm in the air. He began to cut himself methodically, and I watched in horror as he spelled out her name—Hana's name. My chest burned with jealousy.

"See? I'll never be yours, Jackie," he hissed as he finished the last *A*, blood slowly sliding down his arm, then looked back down at me. "But you? You'll always be mine."

He put the bloody knife to my arm and began to carve into me; I cried as the pain seared through my upper half. He began to move his hips, fucking my ass again, as he took a break from my arm.

"I'm gonna fucking come inside of you while you bleed for me," he spit out angrily. "And then I'm gonna slice your other arm as I make you come for me."

I kept silent—I couldn't even scream. My whole body went numb as he came inside of me, the blood dripping from my arm onto his bed. And as if he knew how defeated I felt, he began to rub my clit with his bloody finger. I tried to deny myself of the pleasure, tried to make my body understand that this was not supposed to feel good, not now. But as Michael furiously rubbed my clit, he began to move his hips again, and I screamed out with vexing pleasure as I came under his rough touch.

My body went numb again as Michael laughed and took the knife to my arm. He finished his name on each side of me, and I passed out knowing that someday—someday soon—I was going to die. Not because of him, but *for* him.

# Now

My voice caught in my throat. I heard laughter from the hallway as other hotel guests happily walked past my room and I felt like screaming for help, but nothing came out.

"Michael. How did you get in here?" I asked, my voice barely a whisper.

He shrugged with a smug smile. "It's amazing what a little cash and charm can do." He crossed his legs and held his hand out for me. "Come here, sweet Jackie."

I faintly shook my head and closed my eyes, my pulse pounding audibly through my ears. "Please leave."

He immediately laughed. "Oh, baby. I came all the way from New York to see you. And this is how you're going to treat me?"

I opened my eyes and anger shot through me. "Why *did* you come all the way here, Michael? I didn't hear a single word from you until a few weeks ago." Was that hurt coming through in my tone?

He smiled as he narrowed his eyes. "Did that hurt your feelings, baby? I didn't hear from you either." He shrugged nonchalantly. "But I've missed you. Being locked up all those years had me itching for my sweet, compliant, good girl."

My hands began to tremble, and my heart swelled in my chest. I hated how happy I felt hearing that he missed me. Why was

I letting him speak to me? Why hadn't I run out of the room screaming bloody murder yet?

"Why aren't you stalking Hana instead?" I asked bitterly, as if stalking was some sort of romantic gesture.

He shook his head and rolled his eyes. "Hana is a lost cause. But you, sweet Jackie," he began as he stood up and slowly walked towards me. "You've always been so reliable. So eager to please Daddy. And I haven't fucked anyone in four years; your sweet pussy and ass are all I've been thinking about."

*God fucking damnit.* My heart raced with desire and I felt like passing out with how heavily I was breathing. My pussy pulsed for him, screaming with need in a way that no one else could make me feel. Why was my body so easily and readily able to betray me?

"I'm sure that must be very hard for you, then. Knowing that I'm unavailable," I muttered with shaky breath.

I felt a wave of nausea wash over me—how the hell did those words come out of my mouth? The realization hit me like a freight train. Maybe I was stronger than I ever imagined.

Michael smiled with amusement and shook his head, stopping inches from my face. He placed his hand on my cheek, and I used every fiber of my being to resist the urge to lean into him.

"I don't think that's true, sweet Jackie. You're always available for Daddy," he breathed, staring down at my lips. "I know for a fucking fact that if I slipped my hand down your panties, my fingers would slide right into that wet pussy of yours."

I gulped and tried to shake my head, but I couldn't move. Why wasn't I moving?

"Please. Please leave, Michael," I whispered, my confidence

completely gone.

He smiled wider, then took my hand and pressed it against his hard cock over his jeans. My fear turned into a mixture of desire, guilt, and hatred for myself, because I didn't try to flinch away. Michael was like my fucking crack—I was addicted to him. I hated him, he ruined my life, he destroyed everything good about me, and I wanted to run away. But he was right in front of me, begging for me to take a hit.

He left my hand on his cock and took his other hand to my face and pulled me in for a hard, eager kiss. Tears streamed down my face as I kissed him back and rubbed my hand up and down his shaft. He quickly pulled away, unbuttoned his jeans, and pulled his cock out. He ripped off my white button-up work shirt and then put his hand under my chin, forcing my gaze to his.

"Take your clothes off and get on your fucking knees, Jackie," he demanded, his eyes dark and wild.

I was sobbing now. My body continued to betray me as I unzipped my pants, pulled them off, and got onto my knees. I looked down at my hands that sat atop my thighs, right above my scars from the very man that was right in front of me.

"Oh, my sweet fucking Jackie. Look at me and take my cock like a good little girl," he exhaled, his demanding tone one that I so easily remembered and responded to.

I looked up at him and opened my mouth, waiting for him to thrust into me. My mind was now completely blank—all that I felt was the innate need to please Michael. And soon, he was fucking my face with fury, holding my hair back while I choked on his cock. My drenched pussy ached for him.

He yanked on my hair as he pulled out of my mouth, standing me up and throwing me against the bed. I landed on my stomach and Michael quickly pulled my legs apart with his knee.

"I fucking told you, Jackie. You're always available for Daddy. Such a weak fucking slut," he spit out before he slammed into me, furiously pounding like he hated me; I was positive that he did. I was positive that I hated myself too.

He took my hands and pulled them behind my back, holding my wrists together as he continued to pump hard and fast. I knew what was gonna happen—he was going to fuck my ass and use every hole of my body just like he always did. But then he reached around and began to rub my clit, his fingers slipping around frantically, urging me to come quickly. I screamed out with pleasure as my pussy clenched around his cock and as he laughed into my ear.

"See, baby? You still belong to me. You always will." He pulled out of my pussy and instantly pushed himself into my ass, forcing a painful scream from my throat, but he was quick to put his hand around my mouth and quiet me. And just like he did the first night we met, he forced an orgasm as he rubbed my clit, then came inside my ass with a deep, low growl.

My mind began to race as Michael laid on top of me, catching his breath. *How did I let this happen? I could have run out of the hotel room as soon as I saw him sitting there. Why didn't I? What the fuck is wrong with me? Was Michael right? Would I always belong to him? I just betrayed Elliott in the worst fucking possible way. What was he going to think of me now? He's going to hate me. Probably better off that way—I'm too much of a fucking mess. I warned him, but he didn't listen. And now I just let the man I hated most in the world fuck me senseless. I'm a lost fucking cause. And now what is Michael going to do to me?* Fear slowly crept up my belly again as Michael pulled out of me. I laid still on the bed, afraid to move. I was expecting a blow to the ass or for him to pull me up and take me by the throat. But he didn't do either of those things; instead, he walked into the bathroom, and I heard water start to fill the bathtub. I looked over as he walked back into the room, eyeing me eagerly.

"Come on, sweet Jackie. Let me clean you up, baby." His voice was soft and gentle as he held out his hand. I shakily took it, knowing exactly what he was doing; he was going to try to win me back, to reel me in just as he had before, when he would be cruel one moment and sweet the next. But now I needed to be stronger and not let him consume me again. Except I didn't want that—I wanted to be his. I wanted to please him all over again, to be the person he wanted.

He was right: I belonged to him. I was bound to him. And I feared that I always would be.

# Then

Michael went back to ignoring me after that night. I was almost relieved; the scars on my arms were still healing, and I wasn't sure if I could handle any more pain. I continued to watch as he came and went from his Williamsburg apartment, probably noticing me since I didn't even try to hide it, but he never acknowledged me.

I also found out, through her Instagram, that Hana had married the cute guy from the day in Battery Park. His name was Jack. It seemed sudden—she was engaged to Michael one moment and then married to Jack the next. I wondered if that's why Michael had called me that night. I was happy they weren't engaged anymore, but he still wanted nothing to do with me.

But I figured out a way to get back into his life, whether he realized it or not.

I met Billie one night at a bar near her apartment. I found out that she was Hana's ex-roommate by snooping through Instagram. I discovered the hipster bar she frequented and started hanging around there. I actually liked it a lot, and I began to make some friends since I was there often; those people also happened to be Billie's friends. It was a perfect coincidence.

We started talking and hit it off. She was so cool, artsy, and easy to talk to. One night, she mentioned she was looking for a new roommate. I told her I had always wanted to live in the area. And just like that, we were living together.

I was living in Hana's old room. It seemed surreal to be sleeping in the very same bed she used to. Billie told me Hana left most of her furniture because she moved out in such a rush. She seemed bitter towards Hana, and especially towards Michael. I got the whole story: their wavering love affair, the back-and-forth between Michael and Jack, the quick engagement.

Since I was much closer to Michael's apartment now that I lived in the same neighborhood, I was able to watch him more frequently. But in late April, I couldn't figure out where he was and grew concerned. Had he moved without me realizing it? Did something happen to him? I decided to text him when I couldn't handle the worry anymore: **Where are you? I haven't seen you in a while.**

Hours later, just as I began to believe he would never respond, my phone vibrated in my pocket as I sat at the waterfront near his house. **Not that you need to know, but I'm taking care of things out of town. I don't need you anymore, Jackie. Leave me alone.**

I began to sob in public. Why did he keep stringing me along, marking my body, making me believe he loved me when all he wanted was to hurt me? I wasn't sure if he was actually capable of love. Was he just evil? I decided that I would no longer give him my time. I would ignore him the next time he contacted me; I wouldn't give in anymore. Maybe then he'd realize what he was missing out on. Maybe then he'd actually start to love me.

I considered going to rehab again. I considered going to

therapy. I wanted to put my life back on track and for it to not revolve around someone who hated me. But then, a few weeks later, someone named Jessica called me out of nowhere.

She asked me for details about Michael. I asked her why and who she was. When she told me she was the sister of Hana's husband, I knew it was my chance to get rid of Hana once and for all. I would tell them the truth about Michael, if they didn't know already.

I told Jessica everything. I told her about him abusing me, controlling me, threatening me. I told her about him tying me up and mutilating me, about coming to me again months later to do it all over again. She was horrified. She was sympathetic and warm, even over the phone. I knew just by talking to her that I liked her. She said she would keep in touch, and we said goodbye.

She called me back not long after, asking to meet with her and Jack to discuss Michael. She said he was becoming a problem in their lives. I immediately agreed to meet—I was too curious not to.

Jessica met me outside a coffee shop in Chelsea. I spotted her right away because she looked just like Jack. I waved to her as I approached, and she beamed at me, but I could tell there was a hint of sadness in her eyes. Or was it pity? Either way, she welcomed me with open arms. I instantly thought she was the nicest person I had ever met.

"Thank you so much for coming to meet me and Jack. It means a lot, especially after all that you've been through." Her hand was on my shoulder, and her British accent sounded so sophisticated.

I smiled. "Of course."

"And don't mind my brother if he's a little harsh. He's been in a terrible mood lately."

I nodded and shrugged. "If he's dealing with Michael, I don't blame him."

We walked in, and I spotted Jack sitting at a table in the corner with a scowl on his face. But even with the scowl, he was fucking gorgeous. Jessica greeted him first as he stood, then he turned to me.

I smiled at him. "Hello."

He was cold to me, but I was used to that kind of behavior from attractive men, so when Jessica scolded him for it, I waved her off. Seeing his eyes turn from angry to pitiful when I showed him my scars gave me a sense of satisfaction; I had never shown anyone, and knowing that they were as hideous as I thought made me feel validated. Validated, and then ashamed, because I admitted that I still loved him.

When Jack told me that Michael and Hana were back together, it felt like a hole had cut straight through my heart. But she didn't know the real him. She didn't know all the horrible things he was capable of.

But now was my chance to show her.

# Now

I was like a fucking moth to a flame with Michael. He decided to stay with me in my hotel, declaring he would pay for the rest of the week, and then he would find us a nice house wherever I wanted. I couldn't believe I was finally getting what I wanted from him; I was getting Michael all to myself again—and he was going to love me this time. He hadn't hurt me yet, at least not terribly, so I was hopeful. I had reverted right back to the Jackie he had met that first night in the East Village, and he knew it. He wasn't *asking* me to do anything; he was nudging himself back into my life without questioning what I wanted. But he knew what I wanted; I'm sure he could see it in the way I stared at him and his beautiful body as he walked out of the bathroom after my bath. I lay on the bed, naked as he requested.

He crawled on top of the bed beside me and began to trail kisses on my body, on all the scars he had given me years before. My nipples perked as his lips pecked my thighs and I moaned with pleasure, my pussy already wet again for him. But as soon as he began, he stopped and hovered over me, his hard cock jutting into my stomach.

"You're not going to see Elliott again. Do you understand?" His angry glare struck me with fear.

Not see Elliott again? God, I couldn't stand the thought. But if I was going to be Michael's again, there was no way I could face Elliott. My heart stung—I loved Elliott. But I was deeply, psychotically obsessed with Michael. I knew who the clear winner should have been, but it was as if I was being controlled by a force that overturned all rational, logical thought. And that force was Michael.

I only nodded as I stared into Michael's deep gray eyes. "Yes, Daddy."

He immediately smiled. It felt like I had won the lottery as I stared up at him.

"Oh, sweet Jackie. You have no idea how much I've missed you, how much I've craved you and everything you do for me." *Oh my God, yes.* "To finally be in control again, to have you be my sweet fucking submissive who would do anything for me."

I licked my lips and nodded as my heart raced, my body enveloped with a conflicting mix of pride and anxiety. I had so many questions for him, but fear held my tongue. The first and most important—why was Hana a lost cause? Did he give up on her when she testified against him? From the details she gave during the trial, he didn't hurt her nearly as much as he hurt me. But I understood why she testified against him—I probably would have too, if the defense hadn't deemed me "too mentally unstable." A pang of bitterness surfaced as I remembered. Maybe that's why he still wanted me. He trusted that I would be loyal to him, or that no one would believe me if I tried to tell the truth. A twisted sense of belonging mixed with dread settled in my chest. Despite everything, I was grateful for his attention, no matter how destructive it was.

"You don't need to work anymore either. I'll take care of all your expenses," he continued, then pressed his lips against my collarbone.

I wouldn't argue against him even if I could; the gentle way he was treating me rendered me completely useless. But I wasn't stupid. I knew exactly what was happening—he was going to control me all over again, make me rely on him completely.

But I muttered the words anyway. "Yes, Daddy."

Michael let me hold him all night. I didn't think I had ever been happier in my entire life. My heart felt full, and a sense of warmth and contentment enveloped me as I clung to him, savoring the rare intimacy.

The next morning, my phone rang incessantly. I knew exactly who it was, but Michael didn't let me even look at it, let alone answer it. A knot of anxiety formed in my stomach. I couldn't just ghost Elliott—I needed to figure out a way to tell him we wouldn't be able to be together anymore. The thought of hurting him made my chest ache, but I knew I was trapped in Michael's orbit, unable to break free.

"Let's go out. There's some open houses in the area I'd like to see," Michael suggested after we showered and he seduced me easily, fucking me roughly just as he liked it.

I was horrified when our Uber pulled up a narrow hill to a house just around the block from Elliott's. Michael obviously knew where he lived, so he must have been doing this on purpose, either to hurt me or to hurt Elliott.

We got out of the car, and Michael grabbed my hand, holding on tightly. Was he afraid I'd make a run for it? At this point, he could put me on a fucking leash for all I cared; I was obsessive Jackie all over again.

The high-heeled, Beverly Hills-looking realtor checked Michael out as we walked into the bright house. It was two stories, and the stairs led up to the front door on the top floor. A deck surrounded it, offering spectacular views of the greenery and hills all around us. I could see a hot tub on the deck below, enclosed by a polished wood fence. The house was furnished, and the living room was bright, with huge floor-to-ceiling windows on each wall, giving a perfect view of the neighborhood. The kitchen was white and modern, and down the hall were small bedrooms. The stairs led down to a huge, open bedroom on the lower floor, the entire space bright and airy. I had never been in a house so astonishingly beautiful.

"What do you think, sweetie? Do you want this one, or should we keep looking?" Michael asked in front of the realtor as we looked out the bedroom window, the views just as amazing downstairs.

I felt like a fucking Princess with Prince Charming. It was all too fucking good to be true, but I didn't want to accept that. I wanted to forget about reality and live in our pretend fairy tale world for the rest of my days.

"Um, I don't know, what do you think?" I asked quietly as I looked up at him, his deep gray eyes boring into mine.

He smiled briefly. "You can have anything you want. Just tell me."

I wanted to pass out. I had been fucking poor and barely getting by for my entire life, and Michael was continuing to lure me in with his charm and money.

"Um...I like it here." I smiled.

*God, such a fucking weak, shrill voice, Jackie.* But that's what Michael liked.

He suddenly turned to the realtor. "We'll take it."

\* \* \*

## NOW

Michael was able to put down twenty percent on the $1.25 million house we had just seen. He put it in his name, of course; he couldn't risk me taking anything from him. We headed back to the hotel right after, and I almost had a panic attack when I spotted Elliott standing outside the entrance. *Oh, fuck. Fuck. Fuck. Fuck.* Did Michael even know what Elliott looked like, and vice versa? Obviously, Elliott would know it was him when he saw him with me. I wanted to warn Michael somehow so he wouldn't react and try to hurt Elliott when he inevitably approached us.

"That's Elliott," I said quietly, my eyes fixed on him as the car stopped.

Michael quietly scoffed. "Oh, how fun. Let's go tell him to fuck off." He was out of the car before I could even react; I only watched in horror as he came around to my side of the car and opened the door for me.

I couldn't keep my eyes off the unaware Elliott as I stepped out. But he finally turned and saw me with Michael, just as Michael took my hand and pulled me towards him.

"Jacqueline." Elliott's confused face scanned me before he looked down at my and Michael's interlocked fingers. Then he angrily looked at Michael.

"Elliott. Nice to finally meet you," Michael said chipperly, as if this wasn't the most awful and heartbreaking thing in the world for me—and probably Elliott too.

Elliott's jaw clenched, and he took a step towards Michael. His fists were clenched, and his chest puffed out.

"You're really fucking lucky I didn't bring my gun with me, because I would shoot you right in the fucking chest for what you've done to Jacqueline," he growled, his voice deep and low.

Michael immediately laughed, turning to me and shaking his

head. "Jacqueline? No." He shook his head again, then turned to Elliott. "She's *Jackie*. And she's gotten over the past, and we're looking ahead now. Aren't we, baby?"

Michael turned to me, and my cheeks burned with embarrassment and shame. I only nodded and looked down at the ground, unable to look at Elliott any longer.

"What has he done to you? What's going on? Please, Jacqueline. You don't have to do anything you don't want to. Just tell me the words and I'll fucking clock him right now and we'll get the hell out of here."

He was speaking about Michael as if he wasn't there. My heart pounded, and guilt sank into my belly; I felt like I was about to pass out.

"Are you being forced to do anything right now, Jackie?" Michael asked, almost mockingly. "Tell him."

I shook my head, still looking down at the ground.

"Fucking look at me and tell me then, *Jackie*," Elliott muttered angrily.

My eyes darted up to Elliott's. He looked so fucking angry and heartbroken...and desperate. I hated myself because I was the cause of it all. I wanted to tell him that he was too good for me, that I had warned him at the beginning. I wanted to tell him that I loved him and he needed to run far, far away from all of the destruction I caused. But I couldn't—not in front of Michael.

"I'm not being forced, Elliott. I'm...I'm okay," I said quietly as I nodded.

Elliott shook his head in disbelief.

"No, this isn't right. I know this isn't you, baby. You told me you snapped out of it yesterday, now you need to snap out of it again," he defended, almost pleading with me.

## NOW

Michael's hand tightened around mine. "Do not fucking call her baby," Michael snarled. "She is *mine*, and you need to fucking back off."

I knew something was going to happen if we continued to stand there, so I pulled on Michael's hand and started to walk toward the lobby. "Come on. Let's not do this. Please," I begged.

"Jacqueline," Elliott called out as I pulled the hotel key card from my pocket. Michael actually listened to me and turned his back on Elliott as he followed me.

I swiped the card, and my heart stomped in my chest as we walked in, my tears already pouring out with grief.

"Baby, you did good. I was about to fucking tear him apart, but that would have violated my parole." Michael laughed like this was all a fucking joke to him as we headed toward the elevator.

I wasn't sure what hurt more: facing Elliott or the fact that I was in so fucking deep with the man who hurt me in unspeakable ways.

"I love you, Daddy. I need you more than ever now," I said quietly.

I hated myself as soon as the words came out. Was that true? Or was I trying to diffuse a situation I feared, that he would possibly punish me for speaking to Elliott?

The elevator door pinged open, and Michael turned to me.

"You're such a good girl, Jackie. Daddy will never let you leave again."

# Then

I couldn't wait to meet Hana at the Bowery. I would finally be face to face with the woman I hated and envied from afar for so long. What would she be like? Would she be as pretty up close? What would she sound like? Would she be understanding, and would she even believe me?

I sat alone on the couch one night, trying to read; Billie and I had just watched an episode of *Bridgerton* and I was feeling raw and emotional. A sudden knock at the door startled me. I tapped my phone to find that it was 2:30 a.m. I looked at Billie's door, but it remained closed; she didn't hear anything. I guess that means I have to answer it. I slowly tiptoed toward the door and looked out the peephole. My heart dropped. I opened the door, and there stood Hana in sweats and a T-shirt, with her purse and other clothes crumpled up in her hands. She was even prettier up close; her hair was damp, her eyes were wide, and for once, she wasn't wearing her matte red lipstick. But she looked upset.

"Hana?"

She looked confused as her brows pulled together and her wide eyes grew even wider.

I laughed nervously. "Sorry. I'm Billie's roommate. I've seen pictures of you around here." I glanced at Billie's door, wondering if I should have flat-out told her who I was because she certainly didn't seem to know. And why would she? It wasn't as if Michael would ever talk about me to her. "Come on in. Billie's still up. I'm sure she'd love to see you." I wasn't sure why I said that, but I figured Billie still cared about her, judging by all the pictures of her and Hana that still hung on the walls.

Hana walked in as I sat on the couch, looking around slowly before stopping at the foot of the couch.

She finally spoke. "Um, sorry. How exactly did you meet Billie?" Her voice was soft but somehow accusatory, unless I was just paranoid.

I wanted to tell her the truth. Why wait? But now that we were face to face, I was fucking terrified.

"We have mutual friends." *How fucking vague, Jackie.* I shifted on the couch and tried to change the subject. "You know, I thought you and Billie weren't on great terms." *Oh my God, why did I say that?*

Hana looked hurt, and I hated myself for even mentioning it. "Billie and I will always be friends," she said defensively as she crossed her arms. "Excuse me." She turned and walked to Billie's door.

I mentally kicked myself—wasn't I supposed to put her on *my* team? I watched as Billie answered her door and, surprisingly, welcomed Hana with open arms. Hana was right; they seemed to have a history and bond that couldn't be broken.

I slunk down further onto the couch, my mind racing, feeling like a coward. I needed to tell Hana. I would wait until she came back out and then tell her everything. I felt a little better knowing that I had a plan. I got comfortable on the couch, put on a random show on Netflix, and at some point, fell asleep.

My eyes blinked open, and I jolted up with a gasp when I realized it was morning. *No, fuck—did I miss her leaving?* I glanced at the time on the microwave; it was 10 a.m., well past the time Billie left for work, but her door was closed. Before I could change my mind, I carefully got up and gently opened Billie's door just a crack. I could see Hana lying in Billie's bed, still asleep. *Okay, thank fuck.* I closed the door and decided to wait on the couch.

It wasn't long before Hana came walking out. I smiled and waved a little. "Good morning." I wasn't sure if I disguised the panic I felt. My palms were sweaty, and my hands began to tremble as I sat them in my lap.

She smiled back and headed towards the front door. "Hey, good morning."

*Fucking do it, Jackie.* I stood up and blurted the words out. "Um, hey, Hana?"

She turned and I slowly walked closer to her. I was finally going to do it—I was going to betray Michael. The love of my life. The only person who at least pretended, sometimes, to give a shit about me in my adult life. But he deserved it, didn't he? And Hana needed to know. I didn't want him to do the same thing to her as he did to me.

"I need to tell you something about Michael," I began. "My name is Jackie."

Hana's eyes widened. She looked terrified. "You're...*Jackie*."

I suddenly felt a sense of relief, or did it just make me happy to know that Michael spoke about me?

"So you've heard of me."

She only nodded. She seemed frightened, and I suddenly felt extremely guilty. I needed her to know that I wasn't the enemy—Michael was.

"I was supposed to approach you at the Bowery next week, but I couldn't wait any longer. Especially since you just showed up here." My eyes began to fill with tears as my heart raced.

She shook her head as her eyebrows twitched. "You were going to the show?"

I nodded and began to play with the ring that Michael had given me. "Jack asked me to approach you there."

"Why did he want you to approach me?" She was clearly angry.

"Like I said, I need to tell you something about Michael."

My hands shook as I rolled up the sleeves of my oversized sweater. I glanced up at Hana, and tears began to fall down her cheeks. Did she somehow know what I was going to show her? I held out my forearm that had "slut" scarred into it; I showed her the other side, the one with "Michael" on it.

"No," she whispered, visibly trembling.

I had to show her everything. I lifted my sweater over my head to give her a better, unobstructed view.

"Michael did this to me," I explained as I revealed more scars on my stomach. "He did it on my thighs too. Just here." I tugged down my pajama pants, uncovering the damage he did to my lower half.

"Oh my God," she breathed out. I looked up and saw her hands covering her mouth, tears still streaming down her cheeks.

I pulled my pants back up and I knew I had succeeded—she believed me.

"I'm so sorry that he did that to you, Jackie. I'm so sorry," she sobbed.

"You don't have to apologize for anything, Hana. Michael did this. And I stayed with him and keep running back to him because I'm a fucking idiot. I just hope you're smarter than me because I don't want him to hurt you."

She was shaking her head, hiccuping between her sobs. "No, Jackie. He's a master manipulator. You are not an idiot. I just can't..." She trailed off, staring past my head. "I can't believe he did this. I believe you, I just... I'm heartbroken. I'm devastated."

I nodded. "You have every right to be."

I was surprised when she reached out her hand to my shoulder and gave me a look of sympathy. "I'm sorry. I don't mean to make this about me. Jackie... thank you so much for telling me this."

She reached in for a hug and I immediately hugged her back, relief flooding my body. We both began to cry and I realized that even in the absolute horror show I endured, I took solace in knowing that I no longer needed to go through it alone.

# Now

*What is wrong with me? Why am I still hanging on to every word Michael says? Didn't I learn anything? Didn't my years of therapy help at all? And aren't the fucking scars he gave me supposed to be a warning, a reminder of what he's capable of?* I knew that deciding to be with Michael went against everything my brain told me to do. I was entirely aware of how fucking idiotic and dangerous this was. But I kept on doing it anyway.

I silently sat on the couch as Michael worked on his laptop. All I could think of was Elliott's poor, heartbroken face. I did that to him. If I didn't hate myself before, I certainly did now.

"Did you speak to your boss? Tell her you're not coming in anymore?" Michael asked, pulling me out of my internal pity party.

I shook my head. "No. I need my phone."

He sighed heavily, still looking at his laptop screen. "I'll call for you."

*Oh God. Lauren is going to know something is up, especially if Meg told her about my abusive ex-boyfriend.* But all I did was nod and smile. "Thank you, Daddy."

I wanted to be his perfect, submissive, good girl. My internal dialogue had nothing on what physically pulled me to Michael like a fucking magnet. I could hate him all I wanted, but I still wanted to please him.

Michael turned to me and smiled. Fuck, I lived for that smile. "Of course, baby girl. Come here." He patted his lap as he swiveled his chair toward me.

I quickly stood up and obeyed, sitting down on his lap with my back to him. Feeling Michael's erection grow underneath my ass sent a wave of satisfaction throughout my body. His hands began to scan my body, his fingers softly grazing my bare skin underneath my shirt. My heart began to race with desire as he pinched my nipple.

"Oh, sweet Jackie. Your tits are so fucking amazing. Your whole body is just..." He trailed off as he squeezed my breasts and pressed his lips against my neck.

"Oh, Daddy," I sighed, closing my eyes and tilting my head to the side.

"Your body belongs to Daddy, doesn't it? My sweet fucking whore. You love everything Daddy does to you."

I blinked my eyes open. I was over-analyzing everything he said lately, and I wondered if he was right. *I had to have loved everything he did to me; otherwise, I wouldn't be here...right? Am I that fucked up in the head to like that he marked my body as his? Oh God, Jackie. You really are fucked up. You do not deserve Elliott; you deserve this.*

"Yes, Daddy. My body is yours. I am yours." My voice cracked as I said the words aloud.

"You'll be my fucking servant, my pet, won't you? You'll crawl on your hands and knees and worship me."

I nodded. I needed to stop thinking; I needed his hands on me and his cock inside of me.

"Say it, Jackie." His hand grazed up to my neck and I was certain he could feel my pulse beating wildly.

"I'm your pet, Daddy. I'll worship you in every way you want me to."

He chuckled in my ear and began to gently squeeze my neck. "Good. We'll get eloped and it will be official. You will be my lawfully wedded wife—my lawful fucking property who will do as I say."

Tears pricked my eyes as I nodded again. *No, Jackie. Run.*

"Yes, Daddy. I will be your wife, your property."

He moaned and pushed his hips up, grinding his hard cock between my thighs. He obviously liked what he was hearing, and I obviously liked what I was feeling judging by the wetness between my thighs.

"Mmm, sweet Jackie. You always know just how to please me." He grabbed my hip with one hand and then reached over to put his other on my pussy, covered by only my underwear. "What will your first task as my wife be?"

I couldn't even think—I just wanted him to continue to touch me.

"Whatever you want, Daddy," I breathed.

He began to rub my clit as I moved my hips, grinding against him.

"Whatever I want, hm?"

"Yes, Daddy." I was so close to coming as he frantically rubbed my clit.

"I can feel how wet you are through your panties. I love how fucking wet you get for me, baby."

My breathing hitched as I felt the pulsing of my pussy, nearing my orgasm, but then Michael removed his hand and lifted me by my hips. He pushed me down onto the bed, and as I laid on my stomach, his lips grazed my ear. "Would you bleed for me again?"

It felt like I stopped breathing; his ominous tone sent a cold shiver down my spine, freezing me in place. My heart pounded in my chest, and a wave of dread washed over me, making my body tense and my hands tremble uncontrollably as I lay there, unable to move. My mind screamed *no*, but my body screamed *yes*, overshadowing everything else.

"Anything, Daddy," I answered with shaky breath, although I knew it couldn't be true.

He quickly pulled my panties down and reached between my legs. He began to rub my clit and he breathed heavily into my ear as his other hand wrapped around my throat.

"So pathetic, Jackie. Still as pathetic as ever. Why would you continue to obey me? Don't you know what I'm going to do to you?"

Panic set in—panic and fear as he made my pussy wetter, close to coming. I had to have known this would happen. And why *did* I continue to obey him? It was clear that Elliott loved me, and I loved him. He was a good man who treated me like a queen. So what was wrong with me? What was I doing with Michael? Was it because he treated me like the fucking trash I knew I was?

Michael pulled his fingers from me and slapped my ass hard. "Answer me, Jackie."

"I—I—" I couldn't answer; I began to hyperventilate as tears poured down my cheeks. My whole body trembled, and my vision blurred with the intensity of my fear. I was terrified. It was setting in, yet again, how terribly wrong this all was. The walls seemed to close in around me, my heart racing so fast it felt like it would burst. But that didn't stop me before. Would it stop me this time?

I felt another sting from the pain of his hand slamming hard on my ass.

"What, Jackie? Speak." Pain again.

And something in me began to light up again—my logic. *I can't do this again. I'm so fucking scared. I need to get back to Elliott. I need to get away from Michael.* But the realization hit me like a cold wave: *he won't just let me walk away, waving goodbye with a smile on his face. What do I do?* My mind raced as I fought to keep my panic at bay. *I need to be smart about this. I have to find a way out without triggering his wrath.*

"Daddy," I cried. "I need you. Please. Do whatever you want to me."

I hoped he would like that, and as he softly palmed my ass over the sore spots, I knew I was right.

"What I want right now, sweet Jackie, is for you to get on your knees like a good girl and obey Daddy. Now."

I turned and slunk down to my knees, staring at his brown suede oxfords that pointed at me.

"Look at me," he ordered sharply.

My eyes flicked up to his; his gray eyes suddenly didn't make my heart drop to my pussy—they made my rage simmer deep in my chest.

He unzipped his pants and let his cock spring free and I tried to ignore the aching need of my pussy. Instead, I gritted my teeth and waited for his next command. Then something flickered in his eyes. Did he know I was angry? Did he know what was going on in my mind? He began to stroke himself and bunched the hair behind my head with his fist.

"You know what I want to do, sweet Jackie? I want to tie you up, like the good old days," he said with a sinister smile.

My head shook slightly. *I can't do this...I can't do this...*

"Don't be afraid, sweet Jackie. Daddy will always take care

of you."

Then he grabbed me by the throat, squeezed tight, and began to laugh as I tried to pull his arm away, using all the fight I had left in me. *Today is finally the day—he's going to kill me. So fucking naive, Jackie. Scared, stupid, naive little Jackie.*

The last of my frightened thoughts were clouded by darkness.

* * *

I woke up naked with rope around my wrists and ankles, my legs spread open for display. I couldn't move my limbs even an inch. I realized a gag was in my mouth and that's when I began to sob; my poor decisions led me to this, to Michael who was going to use me in every way he pleased. I even told him he could, as if my permission meant anything; he would do it anyway.

"Well good evening, sweet Jackie." Michael's voice was beside me; he was sitting still in the chair where he had first greeted me. "You look as beautiful as ever spread open for me, your body ready for whatever I care to do with it."

He stood up and slowly walked to the end of the bed. He was only in his boxer briefs and even though his hard cock was outlined through the cotton, my fear overtook any desire I had left in my body for him.

I shook my head as a tear escaped my eye. Michael laughed. "Remember, baby? You don't get to say no to me. You're all mine."

My chest shook as I sobbed. I was grieving the life I was going to lose by his hands. If he didn't kill me now, he'd surely kill me soon.

"Oh, baby." He chuckled mockingly. "Don't cry. I'll make

you feel good, I promise."

He removed his boxer briefs before he hopped on the bed above me and took his cock in his hand, stroking himself quickly. He leaned down and pressed his lips to my pussy.

"Mmmm, so fucking tasty, Jackie," he murmured as he flicked my clit with his tongue, teasing me. "And so fucking wet." He dug his tongue further into my pussy and used his other hand to rub my clit; he knew how to make me come, and my pussy quickly spasmed with an orgasm as the tears continued to flow.

Michael chuckled as he sat up and began to stroke himself again. "You know what I've found to be best at cutting the skin?"

I watched with horror as he leaped off the bed and grabbed something from the dresser. I was certain my heart would stop as he held up a razor blade between his thumb and forefinger. My chest tightened as if the air had been sucked from the room as my eyes locked on the blade.

"No," my muffled mouth tried to mutter, but it was futile—Michael quickly got on the bed again and straddled me, his full body weight sitting on my pelvic bone, his dark eyes eagerly scanning my body.

I shut my eyes tight as if that would stop anything he was about to do to me. My body trembled as I felt the razor blade slowly slice at the top of my breast; the sharp sting of the shallow cut paled in comparison to the overwhelming terror and the far worse fate that awaited.

"Fuck, sweet Jackie. Seeing you bleed for me is one of my favorite fucking things," his deep voice hummed.

I was struck frozen when his lips pressed against the cut and his tongue outlined the wound. I jutted open my eyes as he smiled up at me, his lips mottled with my blood.

"If prison taught me anything, sweet Jackie, it's that you take what you want before someone else does. My fucking deepest, darkest desires became clear when I had nothing but my mind to entertain me. And fuck, all the ways I wanted to hurt you, to fuck you, consumed my every thought."

*He's fucking lost it even more. What the fuck is wrong with me? I could have been happy and laying in bed with Elliott at this very moment. Now I'm going to get tortured and it's all my fucking fault.*

He took the razor blade to the top of my other breast and pressed his lips to the wound again. I observed in dread as his erection rubbed up and down the slit of my pussy. My body betrayed me because as terrified as I was, I knew I was wet and ready for him. *Bad fucking timing, body.* He took his cock and eagerly pushed himself inside of me, his moans already loud and wild as he began to pump his hips as he laid on top of me.

"It feels so much better being inside of you when I can taste your blood on my tongue."

He sliced the top of my arm before he put his mouth to it, and I shrieked with pain and horror. But the friction of Michael's body weight against my clit and his incessant pounding had me close to an orgasm. *Please God, no. Don't let me fucking come like this.* Yet with another slice on my arm, and his body rubbing against my clit, my pussy seized with pleasure. My body shook as I sobbed, the guilt more overwhelming than anything else I felt.

And when he pulled out of my pussy and pushed himself into my ass, all I could think about was the sweet relief of death—but not mine.

*If Michael doesn't kill me tonight, I'm going to kill him.* I was going to end his life so he would stop ruining mine. And it was going to be soon.

# Then

I felt like I had betrayed Michael, but I wanted him all to myself. It was either me or no one. He had already hurt me; I wouldn't be able to live with myself if he hurt Hana too.

I went to his apartment to tell him it was my fault that Hana was leaving. I didn't want him to go after her; I wanted him to do whatever he needed to do to me, and then we would move on. Then we could be together again.

After he forced me onto the ground after he choked me out, after I refused to call Hana and tell her I was lying, he manipulated me yet again.

He was silent for a moment as he sulked in the kitchen. His posture was one of deep frustration—he leaned heavily against the counter, his shoulders slumped as he stared intently at the clean surface. His hands, spread flat on the countertop, seemed almost to anchor him to the spot. After a few moments, he finally spoke.

"Get up, baby. Come here," he ordered quietly.

I quickly stood up and moved to his side. Without looking at me, he took my hand and guided me in front of him, positioning me with my back pressed against his chest. A shiver of anticipation ran through me as he leaned in, his lips brushing softly against my neck. Each gentle, deliberate kiss sent a tingling sensation across my skin.

"Sweet Jackie. You've really gone and ruined everything," he whispered, his tone gentle despite the sharpness of his words.

"I'm sorry, Daddy. I just want you to myself," I shakily whispered back, the lump in my throat threatening a meltdown.

He chuckled darkly. "No, baby. Like I said," he began, drawing something from the kitchen drawer, "I will never, ever be yours."

The tip of the cold knife pressed against the front of my neck, and I trembled uncontrollably, my fear escalating. I forced myself to remain still, my breath hitching as his warm breath ghosted over the side of my neck.

"I would rather kill you than spend my days with you, you fucking nuisance."

I could hardly hear him over the pounding of my pulse in my ears. "Please," I cried. "Please don't."

"I thought you'd do anything for me, sweet Jackie?" His voice was full of contempt and mockery.

My chest heaved up and down as I began to sob. "Then just fucking do it, Michael. Just put me out of my misery already."

My love for him would always be there, despite everything he had done to me. How was I going to live with that? I didn't *want* to love him, but I did. And if it meant dying by his hands just to end the agonizing cycle, then maybe that was what I needed.

"God, Jackie. Would you just put up a fight for once? I can't believe how fucking pathetic you are." He withdrew the knife from my neck, sliding it across the counter before stepping back. I collapsed to my knees, burying my face in my hands as sobs wracked my body, overwhelmed by the crushing sense of how utterly broken he had made me feel.

"What do you want then, Jackie, hm? You want me to fuck you? You want me to keep you here forever, locked away in my bedroom to use and dispose of as I please?" The contempt oozed from every word he uttered.

I didn't answer him. I was lost, unsure of what I wanted anymore—I just wanted him to love me.

"Come on, then. Let's go get your things. I'll keep you here and punish you as I see fit."

I lifted my gaze to meet his. He stood, hand on hip, exasperation etched across his face.

"Really?" I hated how much hope was in my voice.

He simply nodded and extended his hand toward me. Mine trembled as it reached out to meet his, and his grip was firm as he clasped it tightly.

As we walked out of his apartment, he hailed a cab and instructed the driver to wait. Then, he tugged me toward Hana's apartment building. In that moment, I knew something terrible was going to happen. He held something in his hand, some sort of small cloth, and I eyed it as we took the elevator upstairs.

"What are you going to do?" I asked him warily.

He shook his head and didn't answer. "Once we get to Hana's door, act like you're alone. Make them open the door," he ordered.

My eyes brimmed with tears. "And what if I don't?"

He turned, casting me a menacing glare. "One way or another, Jackie, I'll always get what I want. It's up to you if you want to make it easier or harder for yourself."

I looked away and gritted my teeth. I only needed to know one thing. "Are you going to hurt her?"

He scoffed. "Never."

THEN

\* \* \*

I watched, paralyzed by terror, as Michael scooped the unconscious Hana off the floor. My heart pounded in my chest as he carried her into the hallway and went down the emergency stairs.

"You said you weren't going to hurt her!" I wailed, following close behind.

"Shut up, Jackie," he growled out as he quickly paced down the stairs, holding Hana in his arms with ease.

"What are you going to do to her?" I screamed, my voice breaking with panic.

He ignored me, his focus unwavering as he continued downward.

"Michael!" I shouted again, desperate and terrified.

He exited the side of the building and hurried toward the cab.

"Please hurry, mate. I need to get my fiancée some help." He gently settled Hana into the cab, leaving me standing there, rendered speechless in shock. He slid into the seat beside her and the cab screeched away.

*I just helped Michael kidnap Hana. I just witnessed him chloroform that poor woman and knock the shit out of her husband. Jesus Christ. What do I do?* I jumped when my phone began to vibrate in my pocket; it was Billie.

"Billie?" I answered.

"Jackie, there's a fucking water leak in the building. I need you to get to the apartment and make sure it hasn't fucking flooded the place. I'm on my way too, but it's gonna take forever to get there from work." She sounded frantic, and I was still too stunned to question it.

"O—okay. I'll go now." I hung up quickly.

*Should I call the cops? Should I turn myself in as an accessory to kidnapping? No, it wasn't my fault—he coerced me. Didn't he? God, I should go check to make sure Jack is okay. No, the water leak.* My thoughts raced as I took the train to our apartment. Distracted, I got off one stop too early and cursed myself as I sprinted the rest of the way.

I spotted Jack as soon as I shut the door behind me. There was no water leak; Billie must have known something had happened and lured me there to Jack. And when he told me he was going to the police, I knew I had to tell them everything. I knew this nightmare had to finally end.

# Now

Michael untied me and tended to the wounds he created. I was grateful that they were only surface wounds to draw blood; they were nothing compared to what he had done to me before. But this was somehow more disturbing. He wanted me to bleed, he wanted me scared, and he got off on it. He somehow became even more of a monster since our last encounter.

But I still pretended to be sweet, naive Jackie as he bandaged and bathed me. I had a plan: the next time we went out, I would make a run for it and head straight to Elliott. And he'd help me kill him.

I didn't know how it would happen. I didn't want to think that far ahead; all I knew was that as long as Michael was alive, he would always reel me back in. And if it wasn't me, it would be another poor woman who fell victim to his charm. It was clear that he couldn't change, or that he even wanted to.

My heart hurt at how awfully I treated Elliott. Would he forgive me for coming back to Michael? If I could forgive him for lying to me, couldn't he forgive me for temporarily losing my mind to Michael? *Oh my God, Jackie. How the fuck did you fall for this again?*

Michael held me again that night. I wished I didn't enjoy his arms around me, but I did. Feeling his gentle touch stirred up so many conflicting emotions inside of me. I needed to keep reminding myself that he was a monster. He was manipulating me. He was being gentle on purpose, just to treat me like shit again, and I knew he'd repeat that over and over again. And he scolded *me* for being typical. My heart ached as I silently cried myself to sleep.

* * *

Michael woke me up by stuffing his cock into me. As much as he told me how much I repulsed him, how pathetic I was, he certainly didn't mind fucking me. And as much as he repulsed me, and how much I hated him, I still liked it. This only strengthened my decision to end his life.

"We're going to the restaurant. They want you to pick up your last paycheck and fill out some paperwork. Then we'll go do some shopping," Michael said as he and I got dressed and I put on my usual bodysuit to cover my scars.

He narrowed his eyes at me as he stared at my breasts. "Are you on birth control?"

I knew that my birth control pill made my breasts a lot bigger and fuller; I could tell Michael enjoyed them.

"Yes." I nodded.

He shook his head as he slowly walked toward me with his shirt in his hand, his broad and muscled shoulders making my heart flutter. *Stop it, Jackie.*

"Not anymore. You're going to bear my children."

I didn't even want children. But I wouldn't tell him that. I only smiled and nodded.

"I would love that, Daddy."

He smiled and pulled me towards him. "I know you would,

baby. Let's go."

We took an Uber to the restaurant and my heart raced the entire time, trying to figure out what to do. He wasn't forcing me to do anything—he only assumed I'd listen to his every demand. He thought I was still obsessed with him. So why couldn't I just tell him that I was leaving and not coming back? *Because he'll kill you! But what if I got to him first? And he has my fucking phone. I'll use Meg's or Lauren's to call Elliott.* I took a deep breath as we approached the building and let Michael take my hand. I thought I was going to keel over and have a heart attack as we walked in and saw Meg taking an order. She quickly looked over and her eyes widened as she took in who was beside me. She said something to the table she was at and then began to approach me and Michael as he pulled me towards the back of the restaurant.

"Jackie, is...is everything okay?"

*Oh my God, Meg...please don't say anything.* I was grateful she was worried about me though—she had every right to be.

Michael gripped my hand tightly as he turned and glared at Meg. She was probably 5'2" so he towered over her by nearly a foot as he neared her, but she didn't bat an eye.

"Everything is great," he said calmly. "We're here to gather Jackie's things, as well as her last paycheck. Isn't that right, Jackie?" He looked down at me expectantly.

I exhaled a laugh and nodded. "Of course!" My tone was exaggerated and almost comical, but I was nervous not only about our conversation, but also about how I would get rid of Michael.

As Michael pulled me away, I could see the confusion in Meg's eyes as she stared at us.

We walked through the back door into the break room.

Lauren's office was just down the hall.

"Wait here. I'll go get it," I said to Michael, already knowing he wouldn't let me go alone.

He tightened his grip on my hand. "No." He pulled me firmly towards Lauren's office.

I took a deep breath and knocked on her door. *Holy shit, am I doing this?*

"Come in!" Lauren called out.

Michael grabbed the door handle and swung it open. Lauren, seated behind her desk with a pen and notebook, looked up, her expression shifting to surprise.

"Jackie," she began, her voice trailing off as she took in the scene.

My heart pounded so fiercely that I felt as if it might explode from my chest.

"I have something to say," I blurted out, my breath shaky.

Michael whipped his head toward me as I continued.

"I actually don't want to do this. I think I'll just stay here and you can leave, Michael." Turning to him cautiously, I braced myself for the fury I knew would blaze in his eyes.

He scoffed and smiled. "Jackie, don't be ridiculous. You told me you hated it here."

I shook my head and turned back to Lauren. "No, I love it here. Michael wanted me to quit to control my finances, but I think this time around, I'm not going to let him control anything about me."

Explosions of satisfaction erupted in my brain as I observed Lauren shooting an angry glare towards Michael. I pulled my hand from his and crossed my arms as I slowly looked up at him; his eyes were widened with surprise.

"Please leave." I wasn't sure if I was holding my head up

## NOW

high, but it felt like it.

Lauren stood up, her gaze shifting between Michael and me. Michael, meanwhile, remained silent, his eyes locked on me with a piercing glare. Was he actually rendered speechless?

"Get out of my restaurant before I call the police," Lauren huffed angrily at Michael.

Michael flashed me a sinister smile. "You will regret this, Jackie. I promise you." He quickly turned and walked out the door.

It was then that I burst out in tears. "Oh my God, Lauren."

She came from behind her desk to give me a hug. "We knew something was off. I'm so sorry, sweetie. We're here for you."

I let go as I realized I needed to call Elliott. "Can I please use your phone?" I asked, my breath trembling.

Lauren didn't hesitate to grab her phone from her desk. "Of course."

I dialed Elliott and he answered after a couple rings. "Elliott Walker."

I burst into tears again at the sound of his voice. "Elliott. It's me."

"Jacqueline," he breathed, sounding like a sigh of relief.

"I'm at the restaurant. I just told Michael to fuck off. I'm so sorry; I lost my fucking mind," I wailed.

"I know, baby. I know. It's okay," he assured me calmly. "Let me come get you, okay?"

I continued to sob, now with a sense of relief washing over me. "Yes, please."

I sat with Lauren in her office with my head in my hands as I waited for Elliott. I didn't have to wait long, though. I heard footsteps striding through the hallway and he appeared at the door, his worried eyes finding mine.

"Elliott!" I immediately jumped up and wrapped my arms around him. He held me tightly for a long moment and let me cry. I didn't even realize Lauren left the room, giving us privacy.

"I'm so sorry," I said as we finally parted.

He put his hands to my cheeks and stared down at me lovingly. "Don't apologize, Jacqueline. I'm just glad you're back with me."

I knew I had a lot to tell him—and I needed to tell him *now*.

"Elliott, I had sex with him. I'm so sorry. When I was alone with him, my mind just shut down. I know that's no excuse, and I'm so sorry." Saying it out loud only made me feel more shameful.

He only shook his head. There was anger in his eyes as he clenched his jaw. "That's okay. Because now I get to kill him for multiple reasons." His tone was devoid of any humor—he was serious.

And so was I. "I want to help."

# Then

"Full name?" the police officer asked me as I sat in an office with her and another female officer; I told them I was too uncomfortable with a male present.

"Jacqueline Olsen," I answered as I wrung my hands together, then watched her write it down.

Going into the police station was hard enough, but now I was gonna have to talk to strangers about Michael and what he did to me?

"You're safe here, Jacqueline. Just start from the beginning," she said warmly with a small smile.

So I started with the beginning. I didn't leave anything out, even when it stung deep in my chest as I sobbed and told them about him tying me up and cutting me, about fucking me when I told him to stop, about watching in horror as he punched Jack and took Hana.

I was in there for hours, and by the time I finished talking, I was utterly exhausted. The police assured me they'd keep me updated, but I heard nothing—not from them or anyone else. Days later, I saw a missing person flyer. I tried to contact Jack and even Jessica, but neither answered. I was convinced they were blaming me. I feared Hana was dead somewhere because of me, and I knew it was all my fault. Even Billie kicked me out, but I didn't blame her. It was stupid of me to befriend her just to get closer to Hana and Michael.

Everyone kept me in the dark as I stayed on a co-worker's couch. I drank myself into oblivion everyday and blacked out so I could forget all the hurt I caused.

Nine days later, Jessica called me. I shot up from my seat in the break room at work and answered immediately.

"Jessica, hi," I said nervously.

"Hi, love. Have you heard the news?" Her voice was calm and neutral, and I couldn't tell if the news was good or bad.

"No?" I replied weakly, holding my breath.

"Hana's been found. She's alive. They were upstate and got into a car wreck. Michael's okay too, that fucking wanker."

Relief washed through my body and I began to cry. *Thank God. Thank fucking God.* I was angry with myself for being relieved that Michael was okay too.

"Thank you for letting me know, Jessica," I responded after I calmed down.

She paused for a moment. "I wasn't ignoring you, by the way. I'm sorry if it seemed that way. There's been so much going on with Jack that I just...I didn't really know what to say."

My chest constricted. "I understand. Will you please keep me updated about Hana? I mean, if you want. I just want to make sure she's okay."

"Of course. I hope you're okay too, Jackie," she said gently.

I nodded, trying my best to convince myself it was true. "I will be."

* * *

Months went by before I heard from anyone again. I had

## THEN

been sinking into a deep, spiraling depression. Despite my therapist's insistence that I wasn't at fault for what Michael did to me or to Hana, I refused to believe it.

Hana's lawyers were the first to contact me. They informed me that I was a crucial part of the case against Michael. I agreed to help in any way I could and was asked to come to their office the very next day.

I nervously sat in the elegant lobby on the 40th floor of a modern skyscraper in downtown, not far from where Michael and Hana used to work. As I settled into a comfortable armchair, I gazed out the large windows, taking in the impressive view of Brooklyn across the river, its skyline marked by a blend of old and new buildings. My anxiety bubbled beneath the surface, making my heart race and my palms sweat. Each minute felt like an eternity as I waited. I took deep breaths, trying to steady myself, but the anticipation of having to talk about my experiences—yet again—kept my nerves on edge.

The receptionist poked her head out the door that led to the office. "Miss Olsen, please follow me."

My legs felt unsteady as I followed her down a hallway lined by numerous doors. A well-dressed man and woman smiled and stood as I entered a room at the end of the hallway.

"Miss Olsen, thanks for being here," the man began, extending his hand for a handshake, which I quickly reciprocated. "I'm Joseph Anderson. This is my associate, Claire Whitehall." Despite their friendly demeanor, their presence didn't make me feel any more comfortable.

We sat at the large table in the middle of the room. They began to ask me surface questions, like how old I was and when I began a relationship with Michael. I quickly interjected that it wasn't a relationship; it was *very* clear to him that he only wanted a dominant/submissive relationship, devoid of any romance. They glanced at each other and then began to write things down.

"I need to make it clear, just right here at the beginning, that I never had any prior experience in a relationship like that. So I didn't know any better when he began to immediately order me around. He had been very cruel to me since day one." Tears welled in my eyes as I explained, my breath trembling with emotion.

"So then why did you start a relationship with him if he was cruel to you?" Joseph asked me, no hint of emotion in his tone.

Claire shot him an icy glare before turning back to me.

I took a deep breath as I stared down at the table, unsure of what I was even going to say before I answered. "Because I was attracted to him, and he made me feel like I was wanted. I grew up in and out of foster homes; I never felt like I belonged anywhere. So when he told me that he wanted me, I desperately wanted to hold onto that. I know it seems fucking naive and stupid of me to want a man that hurt me, but his charm was just...he was just so magnetic. I can't explain it."

My eyes shot back up at Claire's. I had already decided I didn't like Joseph, so I didn't bother to look at him. But when he asked me about my childhood, about why I was in foster care, the look of concern on his face seemed legitimate after I explained what happened with my parents.

"Did you go through any therapy? At any point in your life?"

I blinked. "Yes. Very often."

Claire looked down at her notes. "Jacqueline, can you tell us about your stay in a facility when you were sixteen?"

*Oh, fuck. Are they really gonna go there? Are they gonna question my mental stability?*

"Um...what does that matter?" I asked defensively.

Joseph answered without hesitation. "Because we see you've stayed in a mental health facility, you've been held on a 5150, that you were accused of trying to stab the defendant. We need to clear all of this up because they will grill you with these things when you take the stand. We need to be ready for that."

I scoffed. "I have scars to prove what he did to me." I stood up and removed my jacket, revealing Michael's marks on me.

"We're not saying these things didn't happen to you, Miss Olsen. We just want to get all the hard questions out of the way to move forward," Claire responded with a calm demeanor, though her eyes darted between my scars, her expression betraying her true feelings.

I put my jacket back on as I sat down. "I didn't try to hurt Michael. He gaslighted me. He wanted people to think that I wasn't fucking in my right mind so they wouldn't believe me," I said, my breath trembling as I fought back tears.

As they exchanged another glance, a simmering anger began to rise within me. It was becoming clear to me that they didn't think I wasn't telling the whole truth. Of course, a girl with plaid pants, combat boots and faded blue dye on the tips of her hair would fuel that doubt.

"We don't doubt that, Miss Olsen," Claire said, shaking her head, contradicting my inner thoughts. "Remember, we are on your side. We just need some background information in case the defense tries to use it against you."

After gathering more information from me, they told me they would be in touch. But weeks went by and I didn't hear anything. That is, until Claire called me one day as I sat alone at the bar, willing myself to drop dead.

"Miss Olsen, we're afraid that our team has decided to drop

you as a witness. There's simply too much in your personal history that the defense could exploit."

I hung up without saying a word. I couldn't help put Michael in prison; instead, I had been an accessory to his harm against Hana.

No one would ever hear my side of the story. With that thought, I tossed back another drink and blacked out into a deep, hopeless hole.

# Now

Elliott drove us west towards the beach after we left the restaurant. The silence filled the car, heavy and palpable.

"Kate was real then?" I blurted out, eager to resolve all my doubts about the life he had described to me.

He quickly glanced over at me as he gripped the wheel tightly.

"Yes. Very much so," he answered with a frown.

I looked out the window, my mind racing with so many questions that I didn't know where to start. When I turned back to him, his strong jawline momentarily distracted me.

"And you're really a therapist?"

Elliott shot me a sad glance. "Yes, baby. Everything I told you was real," he explained gently.

I sighed and nodded. I wanted so badly to believe him.

"But you're also a private detective. On the side," I continued.

He nodded. "After high school, I initially wanted to join the police academy for the job security it offered. However, my mom discouraged me—she disagreed with the system and was worried about the dangers I'd face. So, I followed her into her line of work. But as I got older, my desire to help people, in other ways, grew stronger. That's when I decided to become a private investigator."

*God, he's such a fucking saint.* He quietly continued. "I never imagined hurting anyone. It never crossed my mind that someone might use my services to harm others. I suppose I tend to see the good in people. Maybe that's a bit naive of me, right?"

A lump formed in my throat as I took his hand. I knew he was telling the truth. I could see the evil in people, and Elliott didn't have a single malicious bone in his body.

"I love that about you, Elliott. I really, really love you," I said as I smiled, letting a tear fall down my cheek.

He looked over at me and squeezed my hand gently. "I love you, Jacqueline."

* * *

We pulled up in front of a small but beautiful hotel only steps away from Santa Monica beach.

"I don't want to be anywhere Michael might find us. I can't risk putting you in more danger," Elliott said as he opened his car door and hurried to open mine.

He took my hand and guided me to the hotel lobby. After renting a room, we entered through an outdoor gate that led to several buildings; the hotel resembled an old apartment building. The scent of the ocean and the cool breeze felt like a breath of fresh air as Elliott opened the door to room 33 for us. We stepped into a small room where I sank onto the king-sized bed that dominated the space.

"Keep asking if you're doubting anything, baby," Elliott said as he sat down next to me, eyeing me; I was sure he could tell that I was cautiously watching him. My guards were back up but I desperately wanted him to break them down again.

## NOW

"You really had no idea about Michael when he hired you?" I asked quietly as I glanced up at him. The rugged stubble of his facial hair contrasted strikingly with his piercing, perfect blue eyes, creating the allure that drew me to him in the first place.

"No, Jacqueline. I swear on my life. I should have looked into him more before accepting the job but it seemed so harmless. I had no idea who he was or what he had done."

The angry sting in my chest softened into a feeling that recognized the pain in his eyes—a pain of regret and sadness.

"I'm so sorry, Elliott. I'm so sorry for being such a fucking mess. I'm sorry for not being stronger. Michael turned me into a fucking helpless, scared, lost puppy," I said with a crack in my voice.

He shook his head and took my hand. "You *did* warn me," he teased with a smile.

I laughed and let my body rest on his; he was right about that.

"Seriously though, baby. You are a lot stronger than you think. You could have gotten swept up in his web again. But you made it out this time. All by yourself."

*Is that true?*

"He tied me up again," I blurted out.

Elliott tensed, and I could have sworn he stopped breathing.

"What did he do?" he growled, his voice taking on a depth I'd never heard before.

"Just surface wounds this time," I said so quietly that it was almost a whisper.

His tone remained the same. "Show me."

I sat straight and looked up at him. His eyes blazed with fury and his jaw clenched slightly.

"Show me, Jacqueline," he repeated.

I looked down at the ground before I stood up and began to

undress. There were at least a dozen shallow cuts from the night before, spanning from my collarbone to my inner thigh. Elliott's eyes were glazed with tears as he grabbed my hips and pulled me close to him, then gently pressed his lips to a scabbed cut on my stomach. Every hair on my body stood upright as goosebumps freckled my skin. He looked up at me with eyes burning with desire, his gaze intense and unwavering. "I will never let him touch another hair on your body, baby. He will never get that close to you again. I promise you."

I believed him. "I know you won't, Daddy," I said, my words laced with arousal, as I put my knees on either side of him to rest my weight between his legs. I held onto his strong shoulders and lifted my chest to arch my back.

A smile flickered across his face. "Jacqueline. Are you sure you're ready?" He cupped my ass with each of his hands as I began to move my hips.

"Yes, Daddy. Show me how a real man treats his baby."

His erection hardened beneath me as his lips parted and he let out a soft exhale.

"You want me to show you, baby?"

I nodded and smiled. "Yes, please."

He stood and lifted me with his forearms, his hands firmly gripping my ass. He turned around and gently laid me on my back before taking my calves and pulling them over his shoulders. I looked down just as he placed his lips between my legs, igniting a surprised gasp from my lungs.

"Yes," I moaned as Elliott swirled his tongue around my clit before burying his face in my pussy, lapping around like he was starving.

"Come for me, baby," he growled, then circled my clit with his tongue and stuck two fingers deep inside of me. Instantly,

## NOW

I clenched my thighs around Elliott's head and my body seized with an overwhelming orgasm. The satisfaction from coming without tremendous guilt afterward sent another wave of pleasure throughout my body. Elliott continued to feast on me until my legs trembled and I was depleted of all energy.

"Daddy, please...please fuck me now," I breathed out.

He grunted as he parted his mouth from my pussy and stood to lift his shirt over his head. I watched his muscles contract and my pussy twitched, signaling that I was ready for more. He smiled down at me as he let his cock spring free from his boxer briefs. My heart raced as I watched him stroke himself with one hand, then lean his body over me, steadying himself with the other hand.

"Baby, do you know how much I love you?" he whispered in my ear, letting his lips graze it gently.

"Tell me, Daddy," I breathed back.

He trailed kisses along my neck before making his way back up to my ear. "I love you so much that I'll fucking kill for you. And I'll take great pleasure in it too. You know why, baby?"

My heart pounded so hard that I was certain it would burst from my chest. Elliott's dark side almost made me come from his words alone.

"You're mine now. And no one is allowed to hurt my baby and get away with it."

Elliott suddenly thrust his hard cock into me; I wrapped my legs around his torso, desperate for more. He stilled himself as he kissed my neck, then slowly withdrew and thrust back in, repeating the process.

"Please, Daddy. Fuck me harder," I whined, not in any mood to be teased.

He let out a small laugh against my ear. "I love when you

beg, baby."

His hips started to move and I held onto his strong arms, the feeling of his hard cock rubbing against my clit making me close to an orgasm. He trailed kisses on my shoulder and on my collarbone where Michael left his mark.

Elliott and I were back at the basics, fucking each other with desperate need, only using our bodies to make each other feel good. I loved knowing that he didn't need to suspend me in the air or tie me up to enjoy himself; he wanted whatever I wanted. After being treated like a slave for so long, I knew I deserved something better. And that something better was Elliott.

* * *

Elliott and I lay in bed as he traced his fingertips over my old scars. I nestled my nose into his chest hair, finding comfort in the warmth of his body and the familiar scent that made me feel safe again.

"So, how are we gonna do this?"

He raised his eyebrows slightly; he knew exactly what I was talking about. "I don't want you tangled in this. Let me do it alone. Please," he insisted. "I can make it quick and look like an accident. Believe me, I've thought about killing that fucker a lot since you told me about what he'd done." His eyes clouded with the darkness I had seen only a few times before. My heart fluttered with arousal. However, I wasn't gonna let him do it alone.

"No. I'm doing it with you. Tell me your plan."

His lips curved into a wry smile. "You're gonna be stubborn about this, aren't you?"

I nodded in agreement. "Yes. I won't let you do it without

me." If anyone deserved to kill Michael, it was me, the person he had fucked up the most.

Elliott licked his lips and sighed, then looked out the window and stared at the vast Pacific Ocean.

"Do you know how to fight?"

# Then

*Michael Barnes, editor of local New York magazine, charged for kidnapping ex-fiancée.*

I stared at the headline, unable to tear my eyes away. The words "kidnapping," "Hana Maynor," and "BDSM & submissive" leaped off the page, causing my stomach to churn. I felt an overwhelming urge to throw up.

It had been over a year since Michael was arrested. I had hidden myself away from the world, only emerging to go to work, then promptly returning home to sink into a drunken oblivion. Jessica had attempted to call and text me several times throughout the year, but I never answered. What would I say? What would she even have to say? After a few months of no response, she stopped trying.

Then, Hana contacted me.

I was just leaving work when my phone buzzed in my back pocket. I quickly glanced at it and realized what it had said: **Hi Jackie. It's Hana. I'd love to talk if you get the chance.**

I stopped in my tracks outside the back door of the restaurant. Now Hana was contacting me? Why?

I responded quickly before I could change my mind: **Hi Hana. I guess I can talk but I'm not sure why you'd want to?** I was afraid she would berate me, questioning why I hadn't tried

THEN

harder to help put Michael away.

**I guess I just wanted to see how you were doing after all of this. You have been on my mind a lot. I hope you're doing okay.**

Immediately, I began to cry. Why did I deserve to have someone care about me, especially someone I had unknowingly helped Michael kidnap?

She texted me again before I could respond: **We could meet over lunch or something? I'm free tomorrow.**

I blinked at my phone several times before I typed back. **Okay. That sounds good.**

The next afternoon, I sat in a diner near Hana's apartment. It would only be my second time being alone with her, and I was terrified. What would I say to her? Then she walked in, her matte red lipstick perfectly applied, her long blonde hair flowing past her shoulders as she turned her head to look for me. For a split second, I wanted to turn and run out the back exit. But I waved, and she noticed me and smiled. She swiftly glided over, and I stood up, inexplicably expecting a hug. To my surprise, she did hug me. It wasn't just a polite hug; it was a long, warm embrace where she held me tightly. I began to cry. I hadn't been hugged in a long time, and my body was no longer accustomed to gentle, human contact. Hana didn't pull away; she just let me cry. Surprisingly, I didn't feel embarrassed. In that moment, she felt like an old, dear friend.

I finally let go and shook my head, laughing to myself. "Sorry, it's been a while since someone was so unexpectedly nice to me."

She gave me a crooked smile. "Don't be sorry. Let's sit." She gestured to the booth I had been sitting at.

I sighed heavily, my breath hiccuping from my sobs.

"Thanks for meeting me. I'm sure you were shocked at my unexpected text?" Hana said as she laughed.

I nodded. "Very. What made you reach out?"

She looked down at the table for a moment. "The trial was very hard, and I was really upset that they didn't let you testify. I thought it was bullshit. You deserved to be there; he hurt you so much." Her voice wavered as if she was about to cry. Seeing the pain and sadness on her face as she looked up at me, I almost started to cry again too.

Instead, I just shrugged. "Someday he'll get what he deserves. I'm just glad he's no longer free in the world."

She smiled and chuckled lightly. "Me too. Do you think you'll eventually press charges against him for...for what he did to you?"

I quickly shook my head. "No one will believe me. Why bother?"

She was quiet as she studied my face. "I'm sorry. They barely believed me. What the fuck is wrong with the justice system? It makes me wish he'd just drop dead for everything he's done."

I smiled at the thought. "Or someone kills him."

We both stared at each other for a moment. Her face was serious as she said, "If he ever tries to hurt either of us again, let's just do it ourselves."

# Now

I knew where Michael would be. I wanted to find him before he could find me. A week had passed since our last encounter, and Elliott and I had stayed hidden in our Santa Monica hotel. I had replaced my phone since he had taken my last one, but Michael continued to call both of us through a blocked number, leaving cryptic messages about how I still belonged to him and how I would soon be back with him again.

So I let him believe that. I showed up, suitcase in tow, at the beautiful Los Feliz home he had purchased for us. With my heart racing and tears already streaming down my face, I rang the doorbell. The tears were real, mostly because I was scared, but I wanted him to think they were for other reasons.

My heart dropped to my stomach when he answered the door wearing nothing but his joggers. His body was glistening with sweat, and his lips curled into a smug smile as he took me in. I hated that my body still felt weak at the sight of him.

"Sweet Jackie. You're back." His deep voice was laced with mockery.

"You were right, Daddy. I belong to you. I tried to make it work with him, but you were so fucking right. I still love you more than I'll love anyone," I cried, my whole body shaking with sobs.

Michael glanced over my shoulder, then looked down the street, as if he expected to be raided.

"You know what will happen if you come through these doors, Jackie. You will be my pet. Is that what you want?" His eyebrows were raised expectantly.

I paused in confusion. Why was he asking me? Did he know I was trying to trick him?

"Yes, Daddy. Please," I begged, terrified to my core.

He narrowed his eyes at me. "Get on your knees and beg like a good girl, sweet Jackie."

My jaw clenched but I did my best to appear as the sweet, naive Jackie that Michael had known so well. I got onto my knees in front of him and looked down at the ground. "Please, Daddy. Please let me be your pet."

"Eyes on me," he snapped.

My eyes flickered up to his. The pull to him was becoming stronger, but I knew better this time—I had my guards up and locked, with the image of Elliott and our plan being my saving grace.

"If you come through these doors, you will never be allowed back out. Do you understand?"

Of course I understood; he meant the doors literally and figuratively. And I wanted him to believe me when I nodded my head and widened my eyes. "Yes, Daddy."

He grinned and put his hand to my chin.

"Crawl inside. Then undress and get on all fours."

*Oh God. This better work, or else I'm royally fucked.*

I crawled my way inside, my cheeks burning with embarrassment. I heard the door close and lock and felt Michael's presence hovering behind me. I got back onto my knees, shrugged off my jacket, and began undressing. My surface wounds were scabbed and almost healed, but they were somehow stinging as I pulled my clothes off.

"Do as I said, Jackie." He was angry as he bit the words out.

My body was shivering as I got back onto my knees and dropped my hands to the floor. I could hear the whooshing of blood through my ears, the pounding of my heart practically knocking me over.

"Who do you belong to, sweet Jackie?" he growled, still hovering behind me.

"You, Daddy," my quiet, quivering voice answered.

His hand shot down to my ass, a hard and sudden slap making me whimper.

"Did you fuck him after you ran off to him?"

I expected his question, but I still began to sob before I answered. "Yes."

He slapped my ass again.

"God, you fucking whore," he growled before bunching my hair in his hand and pulling back hard. I only saw his hateful eyes for a moment before I shut them tight as he spit on me.

"Stay," he ordered me like a dog as he let go and walked into another room.

*This is going to work. This has to work*, I kept repeating to myself. It was only a minute or so before he came back with his hard cock bobbing up and down as he walked, and with a leash and collar in his hand.

"If you're going to behave like a bitch in heat, then that's how I'll treat you."

He pulled me upright onto my knees by my hair and quickly latched the collar around my neck. The leash was already attached, and he wrapped it around his fist before giving it a tug. He laughed as I let out a whimper.

"Oh, sweet Jackie, my little pet. I underestimated you. You have some fight in you after all," he began, staring down at me with a spiteful glare. "You tried to get rid of me, didn't you? You nearly kicked me out of that restaurant yourself. And what was I supposed to do, hm? You gave me no choice. Quite clever." He laughed and it only terrified me more.

"I'm sorry, Daddy. I was wrong. I will never try to leave you again," I said feebly as I stared up at him.

He scoffed. "Oh, I've heard that from you before. And then I made sure of that, didn't I? With my name marked all over you, there's absolutely no way you could leave me, even if you tried." He snickered as his eyes scanned my body as he hovered above me; I wanted to spit at him. "I can't fucking wait to taste you again. But first, you need to be punished."

I expected this, but that didn't stop me from bawling and begging him not to. "Please, Daddy. I'll be a good girl. Please don't," I cried.

He began to laugh; I wondered if he was going to mark my body again. I couldn't imagine him doing anything worse than that, besides killing me. But we weren't going to let that happen. I just needed him to believe that he was in control of me again; I needed him to let his guard down.

"What punishment do you see fit, hm? Maybe..." He trailed off before slapping me hard across the face and I gasped as the pain stung across my warm cheek. "I don't know, baby. You take a beating so well. Sometimes I think you like it."

*I don't like it. I don't deserve this. Don't let him play with your mind, Jackie.*

"Fucking you roughly isn't punishment, is it?" he continued, then tugged on my leash to bend me forward on all fours; I knew better than to move from that position. I waited, expecting a blow, as he walked behind me and slapped my ass again. Now *he* was the typical one. His legs lowered to the floor and his finger suddenly invaded my pussy, easily sliding it in. I felt mortified that I was wet for him; there was no way, in any situation, that I wouldn't be, and that may have been punishment enough. He began to rub my clit with his wet finger and I bit my lip to refrain from moaning.

"Jackie, baby. You're dripping for me. Did that bulky dryshite not satisfy you the way I can?"

My cheeks burned again; that was so far from the truth.

"Yes, Daddy. You're the only one that can satisfy me," I whispered to the floor.

He chuckled and then removed his finger from me. He stood up and tugged on my leash, then began to walk down the hall, forcing me to crawl behind him.

"You know what your real punishment will be, sweet Jackie?" he asked as he opened one of the bedroom doors and walked into a dark, empty room. "I'll keep you in here, alone, with only your fucked up mind to entertain you."

*This won't be so bad. At least he won't carve me up again.*

"Please don't, Daddy," I cried, hoping I sounded convincing.

He dropped the leash and suddenly the door slammed shut, leaving me alone in the darkness. I heard his footsteps disappear down the hallway and I began to call out for him. "Please! Daddy!" I stayed where I was like the *good girl* he expected me to be. "Daddy!" I continued to cry.

Only a minute later, he appeared in the room again, the faint light from the kitchen down the hall casting a glow on his shadow. I knew that he was holding rope in his hand. I started to panic, as the sight of Michael with rope instantly triggered a warning in my mind.

"No, please," I begged, actually terrified, even though I knew I would be out of there soon. *I do know that, right? What if this doesn't work?*

"Quiet, Jackie," he ordered as he began to tie my wrists together in front of me.

"Please. Please, Daddy," I continued.

It was dark, but my eyes were beginning to adjust, and I swore I could see a smile on his face as he focused on the rope. I didn't bother to resist—I needed him to think I had surrendered, that I wanted him and would do anything to be with him.

"Fucking pathetic, as always," he scolded before using another piece of rope to tie my ankles together.

My cries continued as he finished, then he rolled me onto my front, my face flush to the floor, and he positioned my knees to force my hips in the air. I wailed as he thrust his hard cock into me, his nails digging into my flesh seemingly with the sole purpose of hurting me. He grunted loudly, his hips pounding quickly against me.

"You don't deserve to come, you whore," he growled into my ear. "But I'll come all over you and let you sleep with it clinging to your ruined body on the cold, hard floor."

His words stung deep in my chest and I continued to sob. *He's going to die. Be strong.*

Michael suddenly pulled out of me and pushed me onto my side, then grabbed my legs to position my back to the floor. His warm cum spurted all over my flesh and I closed my eyes, not wanting to give him the satisfaction of my frightened eyes meeting his.

"You'll remain here until I'm satisfied you've suffered enough for your behavior."

My eyes remained closed as I heard him get up and walk out

NOW

the door. For a few moments, everything was silent except for the pounding of my own heart. But then I heard his voice in my ear.

"Are you okay, Jacqueline?"

A tear fell down my cheek as I whispered, "No. But I will be."

\* \* \*

*Seventy-two hours earlier.*

"How the fuck does this work?" I stared at a tiny little dot in Elliott's hand.

I had just completed an intense, three-day self-defense course led by Elliott, a seasoned fighter with years of experience. It didn't surprise me; Elliott had many hidden talents that I was sure I'd discover in time. Although we still had a lot to learn about each other, that had to wait until we got Michael out of our lives.

Elliott insisted I be prepared for any situation that might arise. Despite my doubts about my ability to handle Michael if it came to that, I felt more confident that I wouldn't go down without a fight.

"I'll place this one inside your ear canal so you can hear me," he said, holding up a tiny piece of metal. "And the other," he continued, displaying an identical piece, "will serve as a microphone. I'll be able to hear what's going on, and you'll be able to hear me."

I looked up at him and narrowed my eyes. "That shit's gonna get lost inside my ear."

He laughed and shook his head. "No. I'll make sure it sticks."

"But..." I shook my head.

Elliott gazed down at me with a look of concern. "But what,

baby?"

*How do I tell him about how I'm terrified Michael is going to do his worst to me? That he's going to toss me around, hurt me, possibly kill me?*

"But what if it falls out during...like..." My cheeks reddened at the thought of Michael and me having sex and Elliott hearing it.

"During sex?" Elliott didn't look bothered at all.

I sighed nervously and nodded. "And if he's rough with me?"

His jaw clenched as he looked down at the healing scar on my shoulder.

"You don't have to do this, Jacqueline."

It was probably the 800th time he had said that to me in the last few days; we had discussed that I would probably have to have sex with Michael to really convince him I was still utterly obsessed.

"I know," I huffed out. "But I need to."

I didn't mean to get angry at Elliott, but he didn't seem confident in me. Either that, or he was scared shitless. "Sorry," I added, crossing my arms.

The truth was, I was scared shitless *and* I wasn't confident in myself. I fucked up everything else in my life—what was stopping me from not fucking up *this* time?

Elliott shook his head at himself and wrapped his arms around me. "No, don't be sorry. *I'm* sorry. I won't keep questioning you. You're the strongest person I know; I know you can do this."

I sighed as I looked up and stared at his earnest, sweet expression; I found it ironic since we were talking about murder. His piercing blue eyes looked at me with such confidence that I almost believed his words.

"How are you okay with all of this? With the things I'll have to do to make this work?"

He seemed to think for a moment. "Because if it means getting rid of Michael for good, then it's worth it."

The amount of pressure I felt to do this right weighed heavily on my shoulders.

"And the code word again?" I asked for what seemed to be the 70th time.

Elliott gave me a sad smile. "Red."

# Now

I lost track of how long I was in that room. At some point, the sun had risen and fallen, and the room was pitch black again. Michael had only entered once to put a bucket in the corner. "I don't want you making a mess of our new house," he spat out bitterly as he set down a bowl of water next to me. "For my pet." He didn't want me dead, but he also didn't want to give me the courtesy of using the bathroom, eating, or drinking water with dignity. He was degrading me and he was taking pleasure in it. I'm sure he thought that would break me, but I had been through worse.

Elliott was in my ear most of the time, repeatedly asking if he needed to get me out of there, but I knew I needed to stay—that was the only way I would be close enough to get the job done.

"Talk to me, Jacqueline," Elliott gently said after a long stretch of silence.

My parents were the first thing that came to mind. Being left alone with my thoughts led me to places I rarely visited, except during therapy.

"I miss my mom," I said, my breath trembling.

There was a pause for a moment before he responded. "Tell me about her."

Her soft features, blonde hair, and brown eyes immediately

popped into my head. I remembered the comforting smell of her as I laid my tiny head on her chest and her quiet voice singing a lullaby as she sat next to me on my bed. Tears pricked my eyes as I hummed along, a sting gnawing at my chest.

"She was very sweet, and she was so loving. I see a lot of myself in her, especially since we both endured so much violence and stayed with our abusers." A tear fell down my cheek. "I never knew how strong she was until I went through all of this. I wish she would've put my dad out of his fucking misery; anyone who hurts people like he and Michael do must be so fucking miserable."

Elliott was quiet before he spoke. "She would be proud of you, Jacqueline. You're an amazing woman."

My chest constricted. I wanted to make her proud by doing what she should have done to my dad. But she didn't—she couldn't. I knew she probably didn't want to break up our little family; even as a small child, I loved my dad. He wasn't a very involved father, but any attention I got from him felt like the world to me. And I knew that you could love someone deeply and unconditionally, even if they hurt you. But this was different; Michael couldn't go on with this any longer. I wasn't worried about getting caught—this was just something I knew had to happen. I had experienced enough trauma in my twenty-eight years to not give a fuck about the consequences of my planned actions.

I jumped when the bedroom door flung open, Michael's dominating presence filling the room. My eyes stung from the bright hallway light streaming through the door frame. I watched as Michael's silhouette glided toward me, his bare feet nearly soundless on the hardwood floor.

"Jackie." His voice was so soft that I barely heard him.

"Yes, Daddy?" I answered in the same tone.

He leaned down to untie my ankles first, my heart racing as I watched him finish before he moved up to my wrists. He finally removed my collar and tossed it on the floor.

"You've been such a good girl, sweet Jackie. Clean up your waste and I'll bathe you in our bathroom."

I sluggishly got to my knees and lifted myself up with my palms. Michael stood and watched as I grabbed the bucket of piss, then followed me down the hall to the guest bathroom. I flushed my waste down the toilet and looked under the bathroom cabinet for a cleaning solution. Surprisingly, it was well stocked with all the necessities. I wondered if Michael had shopped for them or if they were left by the previous owners. He remained silent as I cleaned the bucket and washed my hands.

"Good girl," he praised, taking my hand and leading me out of the bathroom and down the stairs to the main bedroom. The room was bare apart from a dresser and a king-sized bed. Michael flicked on the bathroom light and started running water in the large bathtub that sat beside a window. My stomach dropped as I watched him take off his joggers, then his boxer briefs. Even after the isolation punishment, where I had spent every waking moment hating him, my pussy still pulsed at the sight of his naked body.

He gestured to the tub. "After you, baby."

My weak legs lifted over the porcelain as goosebumps prickled my body upon submerging my feet in the warm water. I kept my eyes fixed on the bottom of the tub as I lowered the rest of my body, pulling my knees close to my chest. I could see Michael entering the tub in front of me but I didn't dare meet my eyes with his.

He stopped the faucet and grabbed some body wash from the side of the tub. He lathered it in his hands before pulling my body close to his, turning me around and positioning my back against his chest. My heart raced as he began to rub my breasts with the soap, squeezing gently. I felt his erection grow on my lower back and guilt washed over me as excitement twinged between my legs. Somewhere deep in my core, I wanted him to suddenly change; I wanted him to do a complete 180 and start to become a decent human being so I wouldn't have to end his life. I had spent years loving him, and as much as I hated him, I would have preferred to *not* kill him.

"So tell me, sweet Jackie. Did you have enough time to think about all the ways you wronged Daddy?" His hot breath against my ear sent shivers down my spine.

"Yes, Daddy. I'm sorry," I whispered into the empty space in front of me.

He exhaled a small laugh and began to slowly slide his hands from my breasts to my pussy. I closed my eyes and was suddenly all too aware of the small device in my ear that was my gateway to Elliott. I let out an involuntary moan as Michael slipped a finger inside of me, undoubtedly feeling how wet I was for him.

He continued as he began to rub my needy clit. "Why did you *really* come back, Jackie?"

My eyes shot open as his fingers moved quickly. "To be yours, Daddy," I let out my panicked answer. *He has no way of knowing—I've been so compliant. He's fucking with you again. Don't give in.*

"I don't think you're that stupid, *Jacqueline*. What have you planned, hm?"

I shook my head as Michael continued to rub me, my climax

near despite how scared I was.

"Nothing, Daddy. I tried to make it work with Elliott, but all I could think about was you," I said in a half-moan. "Having you back in my life just reaffirmed my belief that I was meant to be yours. It's fate. I love you." Tears escaped my closed eyes and fell down my cheeks.

Michael suddenly stopped his frantic fingers and took my shoulders, then turned me around to face him. His dark gray eyes peered into mine, searching my face as if it gave away all of my secrets.

"I love you, Daddy," I cried, reaching for him, but he flinched away and grabbed my hand with his.

He narrowed his eyes and shook his head. "Why?"

I blinked away my tears. "I don't know," I answered truthfully. "None of this makes sense, but all I know is that I love you and would do anything for you."

Jackie from four years ago believed that. Even Jackie from a week ago believed that. I observed as Michael's eyes shifted from fiery anger to profound sadness. I almost wanted to claw out the small spyware from my ear and drown it in the water, to live only in that moment with Michael forever—with a raw, vulnerable Michael who seemed to be just as torn as I was.

"No one has endured so much from me and still loved me. I can't say that I'm even capable of loving you back, Jackie. I want to, but all I feel is anger." His eyes slowly widened as he spoke, as if he had just realized this profound revelation. And my guard began to slowly crack, as if my heart was trying to burst through the hardened shell that I had carefully placed around it, safe from Michael's reach.

"Why do you feel angry?" I probed, reaching my hand out to his stubbled, chiseled jaw; to my surprise, he didn't react.

He shook his head, and his eyes were still widened with uncertainty. "I don't know."

*Fuck. Don't believe him. Don't let one moment of vulnerability and softness overshadow years of his cruelty and torment. This is what he always does—he causes you pain and then reels you back in.* The anguish and confusion I felt pierced deep into my chest.

"You've *never* loved me?" I knew there was a subtle hint of pain in my voice.

I sat in front of him, our eyes locked, feeling like he was truly listening and hearing me for perhaps the first time ever; it only fueled my doubt and confusion more.

He was silent as he stared at me, his eyes devoid of anger for once. "No."

I shouldn't have let his answer hurt me, but it did. The only thing I had wanted for years of my life was for him to love me in return. But perhaps it wasn't love that I felt for him after all; perhaps it was only an unhealthy obsession and a desperate need for his reciprocation.

"But you've loved others?"

I wanted to keep him talking, hoping to find a reason not to go through with my plan.

"I loved Hana," he responded immediately. "And Charlotte."

I tilted my head. "Charlotte?"

He quickly averted his gaze, but a smile slowly spread across his lips.

"I found her right after my mum died. She was younger than me, by a few years, and I was instantly obsessed with her. She was the first woman I wanted to tie up, to hurt. I asked her to marry me and she agreed. That's when I got to experiment—to try what I really wanted." His sinister gaze landed back on me. "Rope. Handcuffs. My belt. She wasn't too keen with any of that, though. She called me a monster. And I went easy on her—she had no idea what I was capable of. And shortly after..." He trailed off, looking down at my breasts. "She got pregnant. I was over the fucking moon. But she wasn't; she wanted an abortion. *Just* like fucking Hana." He shook his head angrily. "It was supposed to be different with Hana."

I was afraid for him to continue, but I only nodded as tears streamed down my face.

"What happened then?" I hesitantly asked.

His narrowed eyes bore into me with rage. The vulnerable and soft Michael was gone, replaced once again by the Michael I knew so well. It was frightening how quickly he could change.

"Abortion was illegal back then in Ireland, so I wasn't worried. But she used an excuse to visit family in France to get one behind my back. She called me from France telling me what she had done. We had broken up, and she stayed away from me for months, leaving me to stew in my anger and contemplate all the ways I wanted to get back at her."

Michael began to rub my soaped-up breasts again, a hint of a smile back on his face. I was afraid of what he was going to tell me next, even though I was fairly certain I already knew.

"I caught her home alone one night. She was just getting in the bath. She never saw it coming." He said the words so casually, as though he were describing a movie he had seen.

My heart threatened to burst through my chest. "She—she never saw what coming?"

I looked down to see his erection growing under the water as he continued to rub me.

"I grabbed the pain meds she had stashed away in her medicine cabinet, forced her to swallow all of them, and then—" He slowly traced his hand up to my neck, then reached behind my head and tugged my hair back. "I spat in her face and held her underwater, watching her pathetic life drain from her eyes."

My breathing hitched as Michael held me back, dropping me lower into the warm bath water, but stopping once my ears submerged and as I wailed, "Please, don't!"

He laughed as he let go of my hair and released me, seemingly thriving off of my fear.

"I wouldn't kill you, sweet Jackie. You're too compliant. You have nothing to worry about as long as you obey me."

I couldn't hide my fear as I began to sob into my hands. *I can't do this. He's going to kill me first. Now I know he's killed before. I can't. I need to get out of here.*

"Oh come on, baby. Do you want me to tell you that I love you? Will that make you happy?" He was trying to comfort me, but his words dripped with sarcasm.

*No. The only thing that will put both of us out of this misery is if he were dead.*

"Yes," I murmured into my knees, my face buried in them.

Pain seared through my head as he fisted my hair and tugged my face up to his.

"I love you, *Jacqueline*. Oh, how I can't live without you, my beautiful, fucked up, little pet." He pressed his lips hard against mine, then grabbed my hips, lifted me up, and turned me around to press my body against the hard, tiled wall. The wind was knocked out of me as he slammed his hips into mine, shoving his hard cock into me without mercy.

"Do you still love Daddy now that you know what I've done?" he spat into my ear.

"Yes!" I answered without hesitation as his fingers began to furiously circle my clit.

His hips slammed harder into mine, as if my unwavering loyalty to him turned him on even more.

"You'll never betray me like the others, will you? You will be my good little girl, my perfect little pet, won't you?"

His fingers were working me up to climax as his cock continually pounded into me, smashing my body into the wall ruthlessly that would surely leave marks.

"Yes, Daddy," I breathed out, my chest constricting with guilt over my inevitable orgasm.

"Come on, sweet Jackie. Come on Daddy's cock like a good girl."

On command, my pussy seized on his cock, my moans loud and untamed for a better and more convincing performance.

As Michael's grunts grew loud as he came inside of me, I moaned in satisfaction, praying with all my heart that this would be the last time I'd ever endure such excruciating guilt from my tormentor.

# Then

*Thirty-six hours earlier.*

I chewed on the inside of my cheek, checking the time on my phone every thirty seconds. I sat on the small armchair near the window, one foot tapping wildly against my crossed leg.

"I can't believe she's coming here," I said more to myself than Elliott, who sat at the edge of the bed looking down at his phone.

He looked up at me with his brows pulled together.

"Are you worried she'll back out?" he asked curiously.

I *was* worried; she had a toddler and a seemingly wonderful life in New York with her husband. Putting all of that in jeopardy didn't seem like it would be worth it. But she immediately agreed to come to California and get this done.

A sudden, gentle tap on the door startled me from my seat. Approaching cautiously, I peered through the peephole. Relief flooded over me when I saw her standing there, arms crossed, gaze fixed on the floor.

"Hana," I choked out as I opened the door; for some reason, seeing her familiar, friendly face brought me to tears.

She immediately smiled and tilted her head at me. "Jackie," she whispered, reaching out to wrap her arms around me. Her hug instantly relaxed my body, reminiscent of the embrace she gave me all those years ago.

We let go after a moment and I turned to a smiling Elliott as he began to stand up.

"This is Elliott," I announced proudly. "Elliott, Hana."

"Elliott, hi." She smiled and waved, seemingly a little anxiously.

I gestured into the room. "Please, come in."

Elliott and I sat at the edge of the bed, facing the armchair where Hana had made herself comfortable. She set her purse down on the floor beside her and clasped her hands together in her lap, wringing her fingers nervously. Her light blonde hair flowed past her shoulders, and she bit the side of her matte red lips.

"It's really good to see you, Jackie. You look well," she said with a smile. "Even though, obviously, things haven't been all that well," she added quickly.

I shook my head. "No. If Michael hadn't forced himself back into our lives, things would actually be really good." I let out a bitter chuckle.

She smiled nervously and glanced at Elliott. I couldn't be certain if his presence alone made her uneasy, but I could empathize—after all, we were about to discuss committing a serious crime, and Elliott was still a stranger to her.

"I think I'll give you two some time to catch up," he said as he stood up, sensing the tension. "I'll be out in the courtyard."

We both watched as he exited the small room and gently closed the door behind him. Hana looked back at me with raised eyebrows and a crooked smile. "Jackie, that man is gorgeous," she said lightly.

I laughed and nodded. "Inside and out. Truly." I wasn't sure if I wanted to tell her about how we met, but I decided I needed to—I couldn't leave anything out because I wanted her to trust me. I trusted her and hoped she felt the same. "Unfortunately, Michael had something to do with our meet cute."

I proceeded to give her the details about Michael hiring him, about how when Elliott learned of all the things he had to done to me, he immediately cut ties. I could see the worried crinkling of her forehead as I explained, but her sad eyes indicated that she felt sympathy toward me.

"And he...he knows about all of this?" she asked hesitantly. "About what we have planned?"

I nodded. "We've already planned the small details, but he's aware he hurt you as well, and he unquestionably agrees with how we feel. In fact," I leaned a little closer to her, "he wanted to do it himself."

She nodded as if she understood. "It took a lot of convincing for Jack to let me do this instead of him. But I needed to be here, and one of us had to stay with Jenny, just in case anything happened, you know?"

"I'm not gonna let anything happen to you, Hana. I'm gonna do the dirty work. I just want you to be there to watch him burn."

# Now

As expected, Michael let me sleep with him all night, even wrapping his arm around me as I lay on my side, facing away from him. My jaw clenched at his gentle touch, knowing the depths of his manipulation. After learning what he had done to Charlotte, my mind was resolute. It was only a matter of time before he did it again.

I barely slept that night, my mind racing, wondering when my opportunity would come. Elliott was silent in my ear, and I worried that my earpiece had stopped working. But Michael hadn't left me alone all morning, leaving me no chance to test my theory. He showered with me and fucked me hard against the glass door, and I couldn't stop thinking about Elliott and what he might be hearing, if he was even still there. Michael hovered around while I cooked breakfast, watching my every move as he worked on his laptop. I tried to keep myself busy as I roamed the house. He had bought the house as-is, so we were set with everything from dishes to books on the shelves. I settled on reading a thriller I found and laid on the oversized armchair nestled in the corner of the living room. But I couldn't focus; the more time I spent around him, the angrier I got. I was reeling since he told me about Charlotte. *Poor fucking Charlotte.*

"Tomorrow, we'll go to the county clerk to get our marriage

license. I need to wait for some documents to come through. We'll be able to get married right after that." Michael jolted me out of my simmering rage, and it felt like my heart stopped beating. *Fuck. I have to do this tonight. I need to fucking kill him tonight.*

I glanced at him and found him staring, as though he were gauging my loyalty by how I reacted. I forced a smile and nodded. "Perfect. What would you like me to wear, Daddy?"

A subtle twitch flickered in his eye. "Well, sweet Jackie, white won't do. Perhaps something black would be more fitting," he said, his smile taking on a sinister edge, one that I was very familiar with.

"I'll wear whatever you'd like," I responded, and I almost couldn't hide the contempt in my voice.

He continued to stare, testing me. "Yes, I know. Go clean up and we can go shopping and find something."

*Clean up? I just fucking showered.* "Put some makeup on. Do your hair. Get fucking dolled up, Jackie. I don't want to be seen with a fucking troll," he snapped as he answered my inner thoughts.

Anger and a touch of embarrassment heated my cheeks. I despised how much it bothered me, but the prospect of a moment of solitude was something I clung to.

"Okay, Daddy." I got up and set the book on the armchair, turning to head down to our room.

"Are you going to be good, or do I need to keep an eye on you?" he asked as my foot touched the first step of the stairs.

I paused to look back at him. "I'll be a good girl, Daddy."

He seemed pleased with my answer because he turned back to his laptop and continued to work. I quickly descended the stairs and walked into the bathroom, shutting the door behind me.

"Elliott?" I whispered as my heart raced; if he wasn't there, I was fucking screwed.

Just as I started to panic, Elliott's voice filled my ear. "Jacqueline, I'm here."

As I exhaled, tears I hadn't realized I'd been holding back streamed down my face, washed away by a flood of relief.

"We have to do this tonight. Did you hear him? He wants to get married tomorrow," I breathed, feeling out of breath.

"Yes. But Jacqueline, I think we need to re-think this. He's far more dangerous than I thought. I'm afraid he's going to hurt you before you can even see it coming. I think you should get out of there. Now." His muffled voice carried a clear undertone of concern, but I immediately shook my head.

"No, Elliott. I'm doing this," I argued.

"Fuck, Jacqueline. I don't know what we were thinking. I should have done this myself and kept you safe," he continued, and I started to grow more nervous.

My chest tightened as I stared at my tear-streaked reflection in the mirror. My hazel eyes were hardened, and there was an unmistakable frown upon my lips. "Please continue to have faith in me, Elliott. I can do this." My trembling voice belied the urgent determination I felt to proceed with our plan.

He sighed before he spoke. "I know, baby. I know you can. I'm just so terrified of losing you. Hearing what he did to that poor girl..."

I cut him off before he could continue. "You won't lose me. I'm gonna fucking do this, Elliott."

I didn't know where the surge of confidence came from; perhaps it was fueled by my sheer determination to finally be free of Michael.

## NOW

He was quiet before he spoke again. "Okay, baby. I'll tell Hana. We'll be waiting."

* * *

Being in public with Michael felt surreal. He had kept me hidden away throughout our entire "relationship," and now he was parading me around like a shiny new toy. As we strolled through The Grove, I found myself continually glancing at our reflection in the passing windows. It was as if I were observing someone else's life. As we eyed clothing in a high-end boutique, women ogled the monster that stood beside me, ignoring their stares. He was undeniably handsome, and it was such a shame that he was such a fucking heartless beast.

I clutched the bag containing the dress I knew I would never wear as we headed back to the house in an Uber. The sun began its descent, and my nerves heightened with each passing mile. It was going to happen soon: either Michael would die, or I would. Perhaps both of us.

I followed Michael into the house, following suit after he placed his jacket on the coat rack. I shrugged off my boots and started for the stairs, planning to hang my dress up to appear as if I were excited about the impending marriage that would never come to fruition. But Michael stopped me, grasping my arm back and drawing me close to him. I gasped, my nerves heightened, as he leaned in, gently cupping my face in his hands. I stared into his dark gray eyes and a small flutter stirred in my belly. *Don't do this. Don't fucking seduce me when I'm about to kill you.*

"You're going to look so fucking sweet in that little black dress of yours," he whispered, his gaze intensifying. "I'm going to rip it off of you and claim you as mine the instant we get back here. I'm going to mark your pretty, wrecked little body again."

I almost wanted to laugh in his face. None of that was going to happen, and he had no idea.

I smiled as I replied, placing my hands to his arms. "I can't wait, Daddy."

I felt his cock harden against my jeans and he gently grazed his lips against mine before pulling away, trying to tease me. "I have an idea. Meet me in the hot tub downstairs, naked. I need to acquire a few things in here first."

*Holy shit. This is perfect. This is so fucking perfect.*

"Yes, Daddy." I smiled before excitedly skipping down the stairs, though my excitement was for something else entirely.

"Elliott, it needs to happen *now*. We'll be in the hot tub in a few minutes," I whispered as I began to undress.

"Okay, Hana is here. We'll be there soon," he responded quickly in my ear.

My heart thudded fiercely in my chest as I pulled down my underwear with trembling hands. Adrenaline surged through my body as I slid open the glass door leading to the hot tub on the deck, the cold air biting at my bare skin like tiny shards of ice. My loud breathing echoed in my ears as I pulled off the hot tub cover and hurriedly stepped into the warm water, sinking down to sit. With my nerves fried, I jumped when Michael, half-naked in his boxer briefs, slid the glass door open, holding a rope in his hand.

He slowly walked toward me with a smile, eyeing the hot tub. "Sweet Jackie, I'm excited to try this with you. I hope I don't go too far," he said, grinning menacingly.

*Fuck.* Panic surged through me, my heart pounding so hard

it felt like it would burst from my chest.

"What do you mean, Daddy?" I asked, slinking further back into the hot tub as he inched closer.

"I'd love to restrict your breathing in another way." He nodded down at the water and began to uncoil the rope as he looked back up at me.

*No. Fuck. Now. Do it now, Jackie.* "R—re—red."

Michael froze for a moment before he burst into laughter. "Red? Oh, sweet Jackie. You know that doesn't work with me."

The light from inside abruptly flicked off, leaving us in the pitch-black, moonless night.

I smiled as I replied, "It does now."

I saw Michael look up into the darkened house, momentarily distracted, as I stood up from the water. I could faintly make out a figure rushing up behind him, and the sounds of a struggle filled the air. The lights flickered back on, revealing Elliott standing over Michael's unconscious body, holding a cloth soaked in chloroform. Elliott looked up at me and flashed a triumphant grin; I smiled back with overwhelming relief.

"Let me get him inside. We can use this," he said, grabbing the rope from the ground, "and then you can begin."

# Revenge

Hana and I stood side by side, eyeing Michael, who sat tied to a wooden chair, still unconscious. We had set him up in the room where he had forced me to stay the first night. A few sharp knives and razor blades were splayed out on a small end table we had brought in, ready for use. Elliott was set up in the kitchen, giving us space, knowing we wanted to do this together. We would need him later, once we were through with Michael.

"You don't have to do this, Hana," I said, gently placing my hand on her arm.

She shook her head, her widened green eyes signaling she was as determined as I was. "He threatened me and my family. He hurt me; he inflicted a significant amount of trauma on me." Despite the tremble in her voice, she conveyed incredible strength. "I'm doing this with you, Jackie."

We both took a step back as Michael slowly began to move his head, regaining consciousness. I waited with my arms crossed as he blinked his eyes open, taking in the situation. His groggy gaze shifted between me and Hana, and a smile twitched on my lips as I noticed the sudden confusion and fear in his eyes.

"Hello, sunshine. Remember me?" Hana's voice boomed in the small room, and I was thankful that she took the lead;

despite my desire for this moment, her presence reassured me.

Michael's expression suddenly changed as he narrowed his eyes at us, a smile suggesting he was anticipating something good about to happen.

"Hana. I didn't expect to see you ever again," he said smugly, the stupid smirk on his face never wavering.

She looked over at me with a surprised smile, furrowing her brows as if she couldn't believe this jackass. She turned back to him and crossed her arms, mirroring my stance.

"Yeah well, I was hoping you were gonna rot in prison. But that didn't happen, so we're gonna help you out and end your pathetic, miserable life. Sound good?"

Michael glanced at her in disbelief before turning his gaze towards me. "Jackie, you're gonna let her do this to me? I thought you loved me, baby? We're getting married tomorrow." His tone was mocking, as if he wasn't taking any of this seriously.

But I didn't falter. Seeing him tied up and helpless—and still trying to manipulate me—only fueled the fire within me more.

I inched closer to him, observing his rapid breaths, and a smile spread across my face. "Michael, baby...of course I'm gonna let her do this. In fact, I'm gonna help her." I extended my arm to the table to find my weapon of choice. As I glanced down at Michael, holding the hilt in my hand, I caught a flicker of apprehension in his eyes. He wasn't taking either of us seriously but now? Now he was starting to get it.

"Alright, fine. Let's make a deal," he said suddenly, casting a glance between the two of us.

Hana snickered and I paused, stupid enough to hear his proposal.

"You two can suck my cock while doing whatever you'd like

to me. How's that?" Mocking Michael was back, and I scoffed and rolled my eyes so hard I almost fell over.

"You think this is a fucking *joke*, Michael?" I snapped, my blood boiling. "You think you have the fucking right to mock us like this? To make light of the fact that we're here to fucking kill you because you're a narcissistic, evil, sadistic monster who deserves to rot in hell for eternity?"

He raised his eyebrows at me and shook his head. As he began to speak, I swiftly raised my hand and delivered a sharp slap across his face. *Holy fucking shit, that was satisfying.* Beside me, Hana giggled, clearly deriving pleasure from it as well. Michael kept his eyes shut, clenching his jaw.

I turned to Hana. "I don't want to hear anything else out of his mouth. Do you?"

She shook her head. "Nope. Are you suggesting we cut out his tongue?" She laughed, looking down at Michael with disgust.

I shook my head as I looked down at him as well. He returned our gaze with contempt but remained silent.

"No, too much work," I began, heading for the door to call out for Elliott. "I was thinking of using a ball gag. One of your favorites, right baby?" I said to Michael, then poked my head out the door. "Elliott," I called out. "Can you go look in the bedroom for a ball gag, please?"

I heard his footsteps hurrying down the stairs to the bedroom. I waited and watched as Hana and Michael stared silently at each other, hatred clear in her eyes.

"Any last words before we silence you, then kill you?" Hana asked, tilting her head at him.

Michael scoffed and shook his head. "Killing me won't rid either of you from me. I've made a mark on you both, physically and mentally, that you'll never be able to escape—"

Hana began to flutter her eyes shut, as if she were falling asleep. "Oh, fucking *please*, Michael." She opened her eyes and fixed him with a steely gaze. "Say something *new*—something you've never told anyone, something other than the fact that you've been a shit person that we'll never think of again after tonight."

He was quiet again, his face unreadable. Elliott came to the door and silently handed me the ball gag that Michael had used on me only a week before.

"Here we go!" I exclaimed with exaggerated enthusiasm, holding the ball gag up in my hand.

"I love you both," Michael suddenly spat out. "I'm sorry. You two were so fucking unlucky to come across my path. Do your worst." His head dropped, and he shut his eyes, shaking his head.

Hana and I glanced at each other. Her eyes were widened and tear-soaked. A sting deep in my chest told me that he was telling the truth, but that didn't make any difference. He still needed to die; allowing him to live meant he would keep harming women. If not us, then others like Charlotte, who never had a chance to escape his grasp.

I held up the blade in my hand and Hana nodded, as if giving me the go ahead. Hana and I weren't capable of torturing Michael, as much as we wanted to. We weren't like him. Instead, I stood in front of Michael and lifted the knife with my trembling hand. I turned to Hana once more, meeting her gaze through our teary eyes. She nodded subtly, her expression a silent yet reassuring affirmation. I glanced down at Michael, who suddenly lifted his head and flashed a smile at me; it was an unmistakable look of pride and arrogance. It was at that moment that, with all my strength, I sliced the blade across his throat. His eyes were now wide open, staring at me in stunned disbelief, as dark crimson blood began to gush from the deep wound. I quickly stepped back and clutched Hana tightly as we watched Michael bleed, his body rapidly going limp, his eyes fluttering shut.

"We should go." Hana's voice sounded like it was a thousand miles away as she pulled me away and led me out the door.

My body was in shock; I couldn't move or speak as Hana took my hand, led me downstairs to the back door, and guided me outside. The next thing I knew, I was sitting in Elliott's car, watching as flames blazed from Michael's house.

It was over; I was finally free from his twisted web. *I will never fall under Michael's spell again. And he will never have the power to hurt anyone ever again.*

## Three Months Later

Elliott and I settled onto the cozy loveseat positioned on the deck in the backyard, a serene ritual that marked the start of each morning. The gentle warmth of early Los Angeles spring enveloped us, eliminating the need for the usual blanket I would drape around myself. Instead, I cuddled close to Elliott, our morning coffees steaming gently between us, while we took in the greenery encircling our peaceful little retreat.

"How are you feeling this morning, baby?" Elliott asked, as he did every day. I knew he genuinely cared about my answer.

I looked up at him and smiled. I ran a finger along his square, stubbled jaw line and nestled my hair into his chest. "I'm good. Hana and I are supposed to FaceTime in a little bit—Jenny wanted to show me something."

Elliott chuckled. "She's going to freak out when she meets you in person," he said lightly.

Hana and I had grown close since the night of Michael's death, texting each other constantly every day and having Jenny join our weekly FaceTime chats. If Michael did any good at all, it was bringing Hana and me together.

"I know. I can't wait till they're here next month," I said excitedly.

Jack, Hana, and Jenny would be staying with us for a whole

week while they explored LA. We promised we would make time to see each other at least twice a year. In the fall, Elliott and I had planned to go to them in NYC.

"Well, if you have some time," Elliott started, setting his mug of coffee on the table beside us. "I think you should take that shirt off and hop on my cock like the good girl that you are."

I would never get tired of hearing his deep, dominant voice telling me what to do. I widened my eyes at him and shook my head. "What are you gonna do if I don't?"

I knew what I was starting, and so did he; he flashed me his bright smile, accentuating his rugged, dimpled chin.

"Just try me, baby," he teased, grabbing my hips as he began to hoist me over him.

I was undeniably wet for him; just fucking looking at him could do that to me. His blue eyes stared into mine, ready to play. I began to roll my hips around as I rested my weight on him, feeling his hard cock beneath me.

"Oh, fuck, Daddy. I love feeling you so hard for me," I moaned with a smug smile.

His grip tightened around my hips, grinding me around his cock. I let my eyes flutter shut as I lifted my chest and leaned back to grip the tops of his muscular, thick thighs.

"Fuck, Jacqueline," he breathed. "If you don't run now, I'm going to take you now, right here on the floor."

*Fuck. Yes. I'm ready to play.* Warmth and heated desire spread throughout my body. I giggled as I quickly hopped off of him, my feet landing on the hard, wooden deck. Instinctively, I let out a small, excited scream when I heard him get up from his seat and head toward me. I ran down the hill toward the lemon tree, my bare feet slipping on the grassy slope.

"I'm coming for you, baby girl," Elliott's deep voice echoed in the yard, and I squealed as I looked back and saw him slowly approaching down the hill.

I began to run back up the hill toward the edge of the yard, but I lost my footing through the short bushes that invaded the ground, and I landed on my knees, sliding down. Suddenly, I felt his strong hands grasp my ankles and pull me down toward him. I screamed again, my heart racing with giddiness, as he grabbed my hips and swiftly pulled down my underwear.

"Nice try, baby. Now you're mine," he gruffed, then he thrust his hard cock into my needy pussy. I let out a scream as he dug his fingers into my hips, fucking me hard and rough.

"Please, Daddy," I moaned, close to coming but playing my part and trying to crawl up and away.

He pulled my hips closer, and my knees skidded down the hill toward his body. He pushed my head down, lifting my hips high in the air, and pressed my face against the wet dirt beneath me.

He continued to pound into me again, harder. "You're not getting away now, little one. Daddy is going to ravage your pussy," he said with his gravelly, breathless voice.

I continued to try to climb up and away and Elliott chuckled as he pulled out of me, then roughly turned me onto my back. His blue eyes were lit up with desire and excitement as he stared into mine, and a slow smile crept up my lips.

"Please," I begged again, almost unable to keep up with our game; I was too excited for him to continue.

He took my wrists and pressed them onto the soft ground, his weight holding me down. He easily slid his hard cock back into me, and I screamed as he began to pump his hips hard against me.

"Come for me, baby," he urged, knowing he was hitting my g-spot just right. "Come for Daddy, and I'll let you free."

On command, I relaxed my body and gave in, lifting my hips, my pussy seizing hard over his cock. At the same time, he grunted loudly in the crisp morning air, his primal moans intensifying my orgasm.

He hovered close to my body as we caught our breath, his lips moving from my shoulder to my neck in slow, deliberate kisses.

"Jacqueline," he breathed into my ear. "Marry me."

I had never felt so safe, so free, so loved and wanted and needed in my entire life. There was no doubt in my mind about marrying him. He knew my answer. He understood me so well now.

"Yes, Daddy."

\* \* \*

Since that smoky night in December, it felt as though my life had finally broken free from its chains. Elliott orchestrated Michael's death to appear as a suicide. After Hana and I had departed, he released Michael from the chair and ignited the fire by setting a candle against the window curtain. Before that, as we debated what to do with Michael, Elliott meticulously crafted a suicide note on Michael's laptop. Just moments before his death, Elliott sent the note to both me and Hana.

Hana and I stood steadfast as each other's alibis, a story corroborated by Elliott. According to our account to the police, Hana had visited town to offer me support during a tumultuous time in my life—Michael had re-entered my life, bringing with him the dark specter of abuse. We presented tangible evidence of his cruelty: scars from the past, the recent cuts inflicted upon me, and a relentless barrage of threatening messages through calls and texts. My boss, Lauren, co-worker Meg, and Zee provided corroborating statements about his history of abuse. It seemed Michael couldn't bear the thought of losing me again and ultimately decided to take his own life.

Memories of Michael often brought a stinging pain to my chest, a visceral ache that recalled the tumultuous moments we shared. How could I have been so naive? How did I repeatedly fall under his spell? Through therapy, I came to understand that my years of trauma, beginning with the loss of my mother and exacerbated by growing up in foster care, had deeply eroded my self-esteem. Desperate for love and acceptance after feeling unwanted for so long, Michael's occasional shows of affection became a lifeline. In those moments, his abuse didn't seem to matter.

But now...now I was learning to love myself, though it was still a work in progress. I vowed never to lose myself in someone else's affection just to feel loved and wanted. Loving myself, even if no one else did, would always be enough.

# Epilogue

I sat nestled in the corner of our lush white couch, reading in my favorite spot. It was a Wednesday afternoon, and I was in a good mood; I had the day off, and Elliott had an early day with his clients. I was all caught up on my Netflix and Hulu shows and was considering a nap. Then, out of nowhere, there was a knock at the door. I quickly scurried over to the window and peeked out. An older man in a suit with a briefcase was looking from the door to the open window where I stood. He smiled and waved. *Fuck, I guess I have to answer now.*

I unlocked the door and peeked at the mystery man through the crack, which I had opened only a few inches.

"Miss Olsen? Jacqueline Olsen?" he asked, his tone warm and friendly.

I eyed him warily. "Yes."

"I'm Ken Ferguson, an estate attorney. I've tried to reach you by phone but haven't been able to get through," he explained, shifting from one foot to the other.

I eyed him up and down. "What's this about?"

"The late Mr. Barnes appointed me as the executor of his will. There are some things he left for you, and I'd like to handle them as soon as possible. His family has been contacting me incessantly."

My face grew hot. *What the fuck would Michael have left me? Probably a box with a fucking lump of coal in it.*

"Uh...yeah, okay. Come in," I finally said, opening the door wider and gesturing him in. "We can sit here." I stopped at the dining table and pulled out a chair for him.

I sat across from him as he set his briefcase on the table and opened it. He shuffled around some papers before piling several in a stack, then looked up at me.

"I'll get straight to the point, ma'am," he started, closing his briefcase before setting an envelope on top of the stack. "Michael Barnes has left all of his possessions and money to you."

I stared at him in disbelief for what felt like an eternity. *No. Fucking. Way.* "This has to be a mistake. I—this isn't possible," I said, shaking my head.

He nodded and picked up the envelope from the stack.

"In his will, he left a personal letter for you, meant to be read only by you," he said with a shrug, handing the envelope to me.

I looked down at the envelope, which was addressed: *Sweet Jackie*. Tears welled in my eyes as I hesitantly broke the seal, my hands trembling as I pulled out a single white piece of paper.

*Jackie,*

*If you're reading this, it means I'm dead. I'm sure you had something to do with it, or maybe it was an accident. I really hope you had something to do with it, because that means you finally fought back. I had little remorse for how I treated you. I knew you deserved better, but I loved having you as my pet. I knew I was selfish.*

*As a reward for being such a good girl for so long, I'm giving you everything I have. You deserve it for being the only person to ever love me the way you did. My bank accounts, properties, stocks—everything is now yours. Even in death, I want to take care of you, my sweet little pet. Do whatever you want with it. But please, do me this one last thing—*

I turned the piece of paper over, my hands trembling. I shook my head, unable to process what I'd just read. "I can't read anymore," I muttered, the anger and disbelief clawing at me. *That fucking asshole.* "I can't accept this. I don't want it."

*I can't believe he's still trying to torment me, even in death. Leaving me something like this, as if he could control me from beyond the grave. It's just another way for him to reach out, to remind me of the pain he caused. I won't let him have that power over me, even now.*

The attorney's face fell, disappointment etched in his features as he shook his head. "Miss Olsen, if you refuse to accept this, who knows where this kind of money will go?" he reasoned, his tone earnest. "My suggestion? Take it, and give it to someone or something else that needs it."

I pondered his words in the silence that followed. Seconds stretched into what felt like hours as I wrestled with my conscience. Finally, with a heavy yet resolved heart, I nodded. "Okay," I murmured, meeting his gaze with determination. With my decision made, a weight lifted from my shoulders, replaced by a sense of purpose. "I'll accept it."

# EPILOGUE

**LOS ANGELES NEWS**

**BREAKING NEWS**
# $3.5 million anonymous donation to domestic violence charity

# Acknowledgments

I would like to thank my beta readers for all of your input and encouragement! I have the best beta readers in the world, truly.

Thank you to my ARC readers and street team—your support helped tremendously with releasing this book.

Arianna, thank you for answering all my endless of my questions like, "Is this good?!" or "Will people like this?!" and also again, "Is this good?!" You are the very best and I love you endlessly.

My family and friends, thank you for all of your support whether you read the book or not. Although, I hope you don't, because I don't want to answer questions like, "What is wrong with you?"

And thank *you* for reading this. I appreciate you and you make this all worth it!

# About the Author

Cassandra lives in Southern California. In her free time she enjoys tending to her house plants, reading, playing video games with her daughter, and laughing at cat videos with her husband.

**You can connect with me on:**
- https://www.instagram.com/author.cassandravega
- https://authorcassandravega.com

www.ingramcontent.com/pod-product-compliance
Lightning Source LLC
LaVergne TN
LVHW011948060526
838201LV00061B/4252